THREATENING EYE

Also by Lesley Grant-Adamson:

Wild Justice
Guilty Knowledge
The Face of Death
Death on Widow's Walk

LESLEY
GRANT-
ADAMSON

Threatening
Eye

ST. MARTIN'S PRESS
NEW YORK

C.2
M

for
Gillian Clarke

THREATENING EYE. Copyright © 1988 by Lesley Grant-Adamson. All
rights reserved. Printed in the United States of America. No part of
this book may be used or reproduced in any manner whatsoever
without written permission except in the case of brief quotations
embodied in critical articles or reviews. For information, address
St. Martin's Press, 175 Fifth Avenue, New York, N.Y. 10010.

Library of Congress Cataloging-in-Publication Data

Grant-Adamson, Lesley.
    Threatening eye.
    I. Title.
PR6057.R324T47   1989   823'.914   88-29901
ISBN 0-312-02654-4

First published in Great Britain by Faber and Faber Limited.
First U.S. Edition

10 9 8 7 6 5 4 3 2 1

1

The police waved him down at the checkpoint. He was ready for them. Name? 'Roger Dale.' Address? '5 Common Close, Harpury, Hertfordshire.' Journey? 'Home from the office in London.' Occupation? 'Magazine editor.'

The constable wrote. His colleague's eyes scoured the car. Dale wore an expression of resigned patience. Inside his head a voice screamed: 'Don't look in the boot. For God's sake, leave the boot alone!'

The constable's pen moved over his clipboard to the next question. Do you always take this route? 'Usually.' On 17 May? 'Not then.'

Dale enlarged: his job sometimes took him to other parts of the country. That was one of the times.

While he talked the other policeman was strolling to the rear of the car. Tiny hairs rose in protest on the back of Dale's neck. The voice in his head argued: 'Look round. Show a natural interest. No! Keep still. Don't appear jumpy.'

The man by his window lowered the clipboard until it swung in his hand. He was looking across the roof of the car. The police officers' eyes met in mute discussion. In Dale's head the voice became a desperate incantation. 'Don't look in the boot. Don't look in the boot. Don't . . .'

Another voice cut in. 'That's all, sir.' The constable moved Dale on with a flick of the clipboard.

Dale delayed his sigh of relief until he was yards away from the lay-by and the men with questions and the posters of the murdered girl.

Mary Cross had been found dead in a field beside the Harpury road near Hertfield. The back of her skull had been smashed. She was unidentified for several days because she was not local and had not been reported missing. Until the photograph of her dead face was on television her family did not know what had become of her. Mary was eighteen, looked older, had left her parents' home in Nottingham after a row and headed for London. She never saw it. She got as far as Hertfordshire and was murdered.

Dale had sifted newspaper reports for hidden information. They said police believed Mary hitch-hiked south but there were no appeals for information about particular vehicles. He deduced no one had reported seeing her in or near a car or lorry. The police did not issue descriptions of individuals they wanted to question, therefore nobody had been seen with Mary.

Two people claimed to have seen Mary herself. A vicar's wife noticed a girl at a road junction near Benfield. Mrs King slowed her car to offer directions but the girl strode away towards Harpury. Another driver thought he saw her walking back towards Hertfield hours later. Both admitted they could be mistaken. Mary Cross was distinguished by nothing but a tumble of thick brown hair and the vicar's wife saw a girl with hair neatly tied back while the man remembered one with loose hair blowing in the breeze. Mrs King described a grey outfit but the man mentioned a blue blouse and trousers.

After a week the publicity slowed to a trickle. Other issues pushed the dead girl out of the broadcast news bulletins and off the front pages. Only people living in or passing through that part of Hertfordshire were constantly reminded of Mary Cross. Her face gazed at them from noticeboards and shop windows. And the police hampered them with checkpoints.

Roger Dale was stopped twice during the six weeks since the killing. After the first time he varied his route but the police were flexible too. They shifted the checkpoints. Sometimes they held up one type of vehicle, sometimes another. At the end of June it was Dale's turn again. He knew it as soon as he took the curve after the straight run out of Hertfield and saw a red Ford saloon with two policemen standing over it. That evening they were stopping red Fords.

'Well, let them,' he muttered afterwards as he changed gear near the top of the hill into Harpury. The country was full of red Fords; stopping those should keep them busy for a long time. And they could feed his answers from the clipboard into their computer and stare at the screen as much as they liked and they would learn nothing. Then he checked himself, warning against over confidence although he could not seriously believe he was in danger of growing careless.

He drove down Harpury's main street of teetering sixteenth-century buildings facing a common. People were near the Red Lion pub and a young couple held hands by an antique-shop window. Otherwise it was deserted. The gaggles of youngsters who usually spent summer evenings on the common had melted away after the murder.

Although publicity had dried up, rumour went unchecked: 'The killer was a dangerous patient escaped from one of the mental hospitals in the south of the county'; 'The maniac was camping in the woods that ringed the villages'; 'The fiend had been scared away from Hertfield and forced to lie low near Harpury' – or whichever village you lived in and feared for.

Dale passed the ranks of Victorian houses, the 'new houses' until a builder hacked down a row of venerable trees and built the eight neo-Georgian homes he called Common Close. Dale parked on the drive of the one with the imitation coach lamp beneath its plastic portico.

His key would not turn in the lock. He rang the bell and listened to two bars of 'Greensleeves' on an electric chime before Sheila got the door open.

'You locked me out.' He gave her a perfunctory kiss.

She was at her most agitated. 'What do you expect? You're late. There's a maniac out there murdering people.'

'One person. A hitch-hiker.' He put his briefcase on the floor, his keys on a shelf.

She was bolting the door behind him. 'I'm in here with the children. Of course I lock the door. They're terrified.'

From upstairs came the furtive sounds of children playing when they were meant to be in bed. Dale was walking ahead into the sitting room, a room the length of the house with a french window to a small square garden. He cared passionately about Caroline and Timothy. He said: 'They wouldn't be terrified if you didn't worry them.'

'I'm sorry.' She was always apologizing. 'I'm sorry. I don't mean to frighten them but what am I supposed to say when they ask why they can't play on the common? Or why they can't run down the close on their own to see their friends? Or why none of the children are allowed out of school until their mothers fetch them?'

Dale had not heard about that. 'The schoolteachers decided to do that?'

Sheila nodded, emphasizing. 'There's a story going round that the police are concentrating on this area now. They're sure the man they want is staked out in the woods over there.' She waved a hand towards the wall with the framed set of bird prints on it and beyond it the Catesbys' house and beyond that the woods. 'There are police everywhere. You must have seen them, Roger.'

He had seen them nearer Hertfield, nearer the scene of the murder. He did not say so. He said: 'Why should they think the man they're looking for is here? We're ten miles from where that girl was found.'

She was wringing her hands. 'I *told* you, Roger. I told you yesterday. He's living wild. He's been moving across country at night. He can't go south where it's more populated, he *had* to come up here.' She sank on to a chair, exhausted by her anxiety.

Dale went to the kitchen but Sheila sprang up saying he was to leave it to her, she was fine really. He went upstairs to say hello to the children and get them back to bed. The girl, who was eight, was compliant if giggly but Timothy, six, wanted to go on playing. Light evenings always made it difficult for him to settle. When Dale went downstairs again Sheila had served the meal.

While they ate Sheila gave a predictably uninteresting account of a day enlivened only by spiralling rumour. All her stories were hearsay. She had not seen a police car for weeks and the details she offered were attributed to a chain of friends of friends. No one would ever confess to making any

4

of it up but someone with a malicious pleasure in frightening others had done exactly that.

Although she did most of the talking, Sheila finished eating first. She did everything with rapidity and an excess of nervous energy. When she was younger she had been called lively but since the children were born her life was coloured by worry. What joy she took in them was outweighed by her anxieties. Sheila had grown thin and tense and her golden hair was scattered with premature white. Roger Dale felt she was not the woman he had married.

She leaped up, apologizing for abandoning him at the table but saying she had been hunting for a toy belonging to Timothy and suddenly realized where it was. 'The car,' she said, 'it must be in the car. I've tried everywhere else and he's been whining for it since he came home from school. He hasn't played with it since he took it to Ashridge when we picnicked there, oh, weeks ago. And heaven knows why it's suddenly so important but you know what he's like. There won't be any peace until it's found.'

Dale dropped his fork to the plate. 'I'll get it,' he said rising.

'No, no, don't disturb yourself.' She was in the hall, going for the shelf near the door.

Dale was right behind her, his napkin in his hand. 'Sheila, I said I'll get it.'

She picked up the car keys. His hand closed over hers making her give them up. He smiled to soften his forcefulness. 'Why don't you pour us both a drink while I go through the car?'

She gave in. 'It's a blue plastic spaceman, so big.' She measured a spaceman between finger and thumb, and turned away to load the dishwasher and fetch two glasses and two cans of lager.

Dale opened the boot first. There was nothing in there that he did not expect to find. He locked it and searched inside the car, checking shelves and lifting seats. No spaceman. He stayed there, remembering the games he and Caroline and Timothy had played while Sheila spread their picnic on a cloth beneath the oaks of Ashridge Forest. The spaceman had definitely been there then, and hadn't Timothy sleepily sucked it in the car on the crawl home through summer weekend traffic? Dale waited by the car until he saw Sheila carry the drinks into the sitting room, unwilling to go indoors sooner in case she thought he had not made a thorough search and insisted on doing it herself after all.

But she did not. She was happy to sit in front of the television with him until bedtime. When they went up to their room and began to undress, car lights filled the space and an engine died. Sheila peeled off her blouse. 'That's Mrs Catesby,' she said and was proved right by a woman's high heels tick-tocking up the path of the next house. 'She's lost her dog and keeps going back to where she last saw him in case he's there looking for her.'

Dale grunted to show he was listening. He was watching Sheila unclip her brassière freeing her pretty breasts. Sheila said: 'The funny thing is, Roger, she doesn't believe the dog is lost. She swears the car was locked when she parked it in St Albans and says someone broke in and stole Rusty.'

He snorted derision. 'Why on earth would anyone steal Rusty?' The dog was not a pedigree animal. He was old and lame.

'I don't know. I'm just telling you what Mrs Catesby says. She thinks . . .'

But he was not interested in Mrs Catesby, a middle-aged woman with a dull husband who worked abroad for long spells. As Sheila stepped out of her skirt he drew her to him, crushing her breasts against his skin.

Pauline Williams was not the secretary Roger Dale would have chosen. She had come with the job. She was intelligent, efficient and had a pleasant manner. But she also had heavy features and heavier legs. He did not find her sexually exciting.

Neither had he made any effort to hide his opinion and she had endured the humiliation of his attempt to persuade the personnel officer to swap her for a pretty blonde who had joined the company. Pauline, at twenty-nine, was mature enough to survive his unfortunate behaviour but the episode had far-reaching effects. She could not judge how much she was influenced by a subconscious desire for revenge.

She had, at the time, thought about resigning but the office was otherwise congenial and, never one for rash decisions, she let time drift by. A vague ambition to brighten her life by working abroad remained a fantasy. Her hope that Dale, like his predecessors, would quickly move on was unfulfilled.

On the morning after Dale was stopped by the police for the second time, he was very late into the office. Pauline opened the post. Normally Dale did this himself unless he was working away. Several times he had mentioned to her, with casual insistence, that she was to be careful not to open the personal letters occasionally sent to him at the office. There had been envelopes marked with his name and the address but no reference to either the magazine, *Pinboard*, or the company, Brigges. She had, without comment, set them untouched on his desk beside the framed photograph of his children.

The day Dale was late, Pauline saw something which set her on a long trail of suspicion. Alone, she would have been alerted by the truncated address and put the letter aside. But Marion Fox, secretary to the press officer, was with her and they were talking. Or Marion was. She had a startling tale about conflict among the upper echelons at Brigges and when Marion was told anything in confidence she interpreted that to mean she was entitled to share it with Pauline. So while Pauline's mind was on the coup on the sixth floor, her fingers slid the knife along a white envelope and out came a handwritten letter from a girl offering herself as a photographic model.

Marion's tale foundered as Pauline stiffened. She went round the desk to read over her shoulder. 'This is disgusting!' she said, plucking it from Pauline's hand to savour the disgusting thing a second time.

'It must be a mistake,' suggested Pauline.

'What mistake? Listen.' Marion struck a pose. She was a bouncily overweight woman of twenty-four who wore tight leather belts. Someone had told her she looked like Ruth James, an actress in a television soap opera, and Marion had taken to dressing and behaving as much as possible like the character Ruth James played. She cleared her throat and read out. ' "Dear Mr Dales . . ." '

'Well, *that* mistake,' Pauline insisted. 'The name's not precisely Roger's, is it?'

Marion gave her a pitying look and went on: ' "I am writing to offer my services as a model for your glamour photography. I have a little experience and no objection to nude." '

Pauline hushed her. Someone was in the corridor. Footsteps passed. In a lower voice Marion read the rest. The writer said she was sixteen and gave her measurements. She promised a photograph if Mr Dales cared to write to her in West London.

Marion hissed a few more times that it was disgusting and then went, leaving Pauline with the problem of what to do with the letter. Unlike Marion she thought it none of her business if Roger Dale's hobby was 'glamour photography'. And he had tried to keep it from her. It had never been his intention to upset or embarrass her by letting the personal mail he could not direct to his home fall into her hands.

She toyed with Marion's suggestion of throwing the letter away and tried to convince herself she would be protecting a foolish girl by doing so. Yet the girl had already done work of that sort. Pauline dismissed that argument. She looked for another way, a way that would not put her in the wrong as firmly as would destroying someone else's letter.

After a moment she hid the letter and envelope in her handbag and went to a stationery cupboard where she found a stock of small, plain, white envelopes which, unlike the newer ones, did not have the company's name printed on them. She used the nearest typewriter to address the envelope in the manner the girl had handwritten the original. There would be no stamp or Post Office frank on the substitute as though it had been pushed through the letter box overnight. Pauline sealed the letter in its fresh envelope and left it on Dale's desk.

Scrupulously honest, she was not happy about any of this but could think of no other method which would have prevented Dale knowing she had discovered him. A thrown-away letter might be succeeded by another from the girl and unless it was intercepted too Dale would suspect her. But this way she could control the situation and conceal it.

She did not confide in Marion but urged her not to tell anyone about the letter and had to trust her promise. Unattached, Pauline had the self reliance of those whose decisions are habitually solitary. Her flatmate, the one friend she might have confided in, was in hospital. Pauline had nursed Jane at home until her condition deteriorated and the doctor ordered an ambulance. Jane's illness was to last most of that summer, and so it was that in the difficult days ahead of her Pauline was more isolated than usual.

Dale was late because he stopped in Hertfield on his way to work and when he continued the journey he was trapped at another police checkpoint. Unlike the previous evening, he had to join a queue. Someone ahead of him was held up for a long while. The vehicles were not all red Fords but a cross section which might have been picked at random from the flow of southbound traffic.

He sat calmly and listened to the car radio while he waited. It did not matter now if anybody inspected the boot. He had emptied it in Hertfield.

The police who eventually questioned him were not those he had seen before. He repeated his earlier answers. While he did so two officers looked at the car in detail, one brushing dust off paintwork near a rear light. They asked to see in the boot and he handed over his keys. He stayed in his seat, his rear view in the interior mirror obliterated as the boot lid was raised. The man beside him was still asking questions. Had be been here, had he been there, at what times did he travel on the Harpury road, was he certain he had been in Sheffield on 17 May, could he have the date wrong?

The boot lid slammed. He was free to go. He pulled forward, pausing at the end of the lay-by for a gap in the traffic. The police were now surrounding a van and the driver was getting out to talk to them. Further down the queue two other drivers were stretching their legs.

With chilling certainty Dale knew why he had been waved down. The vehicles were random but the drivers had something in common. They were all bearded men with brown hair.

His hands were clammy, letting the steering wheel slide in his grip as he moved off. A horn sounded an aggressive warning before he steadied his car. He drove automatically, unable to concentrate on anything but the shock. *Someone had seen him at the scene of the murder.* Someone must have done, because the police knew the type of car that had been there and what its driver looked like.

In the weeks since the killing his hope of avoiding discovery had strengthened but now it looked as though a witness had gone, belatedly, to the police. He was afraid.

When he reached the office Pauline was busy and broke off only long enough to give him some telephone messages and hear his explanation for being delayed. He would not have mentioned the checkpoint but Ralph Gough, the crinkly-haired Scots press officer, looked in to say somebody he knew had been held up at one on that road. Dale stuffed the unopened letter into his pocket while they talked. Then he settled down to write a feature, thankful that Pauline was the mousy type who did not expect much of his attention. It amused him that Gough described her as deep, meaning that there was a more interesting personality hidden behind the dull exterior. He did not believe there was.

But just then Pauline was entertained by a new and horrifying idea that linked Dale to the murder. The letter revealed an unsavoury side to his nature and it was only a short hop for her to imagine that he might not only photograph women, that perhaps Mary Cross had resisted whatever else he wanted. She curbed herself, she was going much too far. It was possible the letter was never intended for Roger Dale but for a Mr Dales who had become confused with him. In any event, nude photographs and murders were not of the same order and she had never know Dale violent.

Even so, Pauline looked through the desk diary to check where he had been when the murder took place. What she read might have laid the matter to rest because Dale had been to Brigges's Sheffield factory and stayed away for two nights, 16 and 17 May.

The information made her feel foolish. The thought had been fluttering in her mind that she should tell the police her suspicion, and how rash that would have been when she ought to have known he was in Yorkshire when Mary Cross died! A flush crept up her neck. With an honesty that did her credit, she asked herself whether she had truly believed Dale a serious suspect or whether she had not wanted him humiliated by being linked with the case and having his secret hobby exposed. Yes, she thought, it was likely she had spotted a means of revenge for his rejection of her, a rejection which would have hurt far less had she not once found him attractive.

She lunched at a wine bar with Marion who retailed a fresh skirmish in the office coup. The pathetic letter to Dale was not mentioned. On their way back to work Marion bought an early edition of the evening paper, something she occasionally did if a headline caught her eye. This time it was the front-page picture which drew her. 'Look at that, Pauline!'

It was a photofit issued by the police seeking Mary Cross's killer. It looked very like Roger Dale.

2

Jeffrey Miles was plotting his escape from Benfield vicarage. When he had started work at the church he had been glad of a room but the attraction had palled. It was still pleasant to open his eyes in the morning to the view of a wood a few yards from his ground-floor window, he liked the way the church clock shaped his days and unwaking nights, and he was happy working in St John's. The trouble was Jenny.

Jenny King, the wife of the vicar of Benfield, was friendly and outgoing, an entirely modern young woman in her twenties. Miles found this difficult to deal with. He liked his own company best and nourished an unreasonable resentment of her kindness.

He had arrived on a damp May Day to the anachronistic sight of grown men in bells dancing around a maypole on the village green. 'All my wife's doing,' said the Reverend Adam King with a laugh as he shook hands with Miles and took in the younger man's neat casual outfit, the direct look from the grey eyes. He did not need to add that if his wife had not been loved by everyone in the village this could never have happened. 'I'm not convinced the vicarage ought to encourage the survival of pagan performance but Jenny said the green was wasted without a bit of this.'

'She's got the day wrong,' said Miles unsmiling. 'The old May Day was six days later. They changed the calendar.'

'Well, don't tell her or she'll want them to come back next week.' King gave another laugh. Rain had flattened his fine brown hair so that the prominent forehead and deep-set blue eyes were exaggerated. There was a comfortable shabbiness about the waterproof jacket which hung open, revealing his clerical collar. Miles's first, inadequate impression was that he was a relaxed and contented man.

He did not answer. He watched the dancers, congratulating themselves at the end of their dance, conferring about what to offer their audience next. In a hoop around them stood the villagers and people from other places in the parish, two hundred who had not minded the wet grass underfoot and the hazard of more showers to come.

The green was roughly oval with cottages scattered around its perimeter and, on the south side, a lane curving west. Car owners living on the north of the green took a cavalier attitude to a ban on vehicles and parked on the grass near their front doors. Fields rolled south in the direction of Hertfield and trees filled the other views.

The vicar and Miles walked to the church, Miles eager to see it and King hardly believing his luck at finding a skilled man prepared to consider the job for a paltry fee. After Church Cottages, a string of brick and flint houses on the north–south road, and opposite a bus stop there came in sight the gateway to the vicarage and immediately beyond it the path to the church.

St John's lay back from the road, a brindled building of grey stone, knapped flint and Roman brick. Rust stained the clock face on the squat tower and guttering sagged. The exterior was unexceptional, just another English country church in a graveyard of lichen-covered stones.

As they climbed the path up the rise to the church, King suffered his first misgivings. Supposing Miles did not think the job worth his while? Suppose he said the carvings were nothing special? King steeled himself to apologize, knowing it would sound lame to blame the enthusiasm of his wife's architect cousin, Donald Gill, who had urged him to get the carvings cleaned up.

They went into the porch and King twisted the heavy ring latch. There was a satisfying antiquity in the heaviness of the door, a promise in the carved decoration around it. He saw Miles run his eyes over the stonework. Then they were inside, vision adjusting to comparative darkness.

'Up here,' said King, his voice fractionally too loud. Jenny teased him that only clergy, the most reverent of men, were free to shout in church.

Silent, Miles followed and they stood side by side while King pointed out, below the great timbers of the roof of the nave, medieval carvings that someone had once chosen to plaster over. Another incumbent had succumbed to curiosity and stripped three but why he had not also tackled the rest of the row of amorphous protrusions no one could say.

Donald Gill, full of youthful exuberance, had run a ladder up against the wall and shouted down that the three were 'superb' and the rest 'must be done'. He had promised to see whether, through his professional contacts, he could track down someone who would do the work cheaply and could be trusted not to cause damage. Gill's scheme had gathered a momentum of its own and King had been told Miles was on his way.

Miles said nothing, gazing up at the exposed figures. The vicar's hopes dwindled. He feared it had been a mistake. Miles's continued silence troubled him. King spoke once more, unable to prevent himself in his impatience to provoke a response. Better to get the awkward refusal over, he thought, than drag things out and end up just the same with Miles carrying his bag back to the bus stop and the episode written off as misplaced enthusiasm by a young incumbent determined to prove there was something special about his church.

King said: 'We think they're saints. Presumably the other panels would turn out to be more of them. If it's at all worth your effort, there's a ladder somewhere . . .'

Miles was still looking up. King's words died slowly in the morning. He waited for Miles. Finally King cleared his throat and said: 'Look, if it's no good say so. You mustn't feel obliged to go any further with this if it's not what you . . .'

'Fetch the ladder,' said Miles.

Mounting it, Miles had been suffused with excitement. He could not understand the vicar practically willing him to reject the carvings. He climbed, face upturned to focus on the stone. Each carving was set in a panel. Each panel depicted a scene in the life of a saint. The plaster that had concealed them had been painstakingly gouged from around figures, flowers and animals.

Below him Miles heard King's feet shuffle on stone slabs. He had forgotten the vicar was there as he let his mind be transported to the time when a medieval craftsman had worked the stone into decoration fit for his Lord's house. Miles ignored King a while longer and let his imagination play with the detail of making and fixing the panels before shifting forward through the centuries to the tranquil hours he could, if he wished, spend in St John's bringing the others back to life.

He liked being up there with them. He pictured a platform and long undisturbed summer days. Reluctantly he went back to ground level.

'Well?' asked King, one hand steadying the ladder.

'I'll need a platform,' Miles said.

King's face had broken into an unrestrained smile. 'Oh, I'm *so* glad you'll come.' And at the time he had been.

Jenny had run in then, wearing a one-piece magenta outfit that Miles had noticed among the watchers on the village green. It started like a blouse and ended in trousers, a matching cotton belt emphasizing the slimness of her waist. He thought it might be called a tracksuit or a jumpsuit but was vague about such things. Jenny learned the news from her husband's face and her pleasure equalled his. Miles thought for a startled instant that she was going to throw her arms around him. Instead she ushered him to the vicarage where she made him lunch and the offer of a room.

She suggested the room would be convenient but he knew she was also thinking of the money. He was not going to be paid much but let them understand it suited him to occupy himself at St John's before an engagement in the West Country some weeks ahead. Jenny wanted to know more but he was vague, saying it was not finalized and he dare not tempt fate by talking about it.

She had shown him the room. 'It's downstairs and there's a shower room next door.'

He had looked around the square Georgian room with sparse furniture and floor-length windows facing the lawn.

The lawn was broken by shrubs and then the trees began. He told Jenny it was a very nice room.

'I'm afraid I haven't got around to curtains,' she said, 'but these work.' She unfolded shutters.

Jenny had left him then and he had put his grey bag unpacked in the wall cupboard and pushed up the bottom of a window. Wet grass shone, raindrops flashed on fresh young leaves and nest-building birds called among the trees. A vicarage cat, fur darkening with moisture, slunk into the wood.

Miles grew to love that wood, to waking each morning and discovering it. He never used the shutters. He believed he had never been so happy. But a couple of months later he was plotting to escape from the vicarage.

The realization that he must leave crept over him gradually, but once he had recognized it his going was inevitable. He could cope during the day when people visited the church because he was physically cut off from them and it was possible some never discovered him on the platform, but in the evenings he felt, quite unfairly, that his privacy could be shattered at any time by Jenny's tap on his door with an invitation to join in whatever was going on in the house. If ever she did call he excused himself by saying he was reading, although that had encouraged her to seek out books to interest him. Eager for company herself, she offered him too much. So he had to move out.

That presented a difficulty. Wherever he went to live would be expensive. The Kings had the idea that he did not care about the low fee for his work at St John's because he had savings or a private income which allowed him to be casual about money. This was not true but he had not corrected them because it would have raised questions. Besides, it was amusing that a misconception eased their consciences about what they paid him.

Once he had made up his mind to go he was impatient to be out. He schemed all day Tuesday and was still worrying at it when Jenny brought a mug of coffee into the church for him next morning. In the beginning he had gone to the vicarage for his coffee but rather than be hooked into conversation with either of the Kings he had been prepared to go without a drink. To his annoyance Jenny's kind response had been to deliver it to him.

He gave scant attention to what she was saying about having trouble with her car and this being awkward because she wanted to visit Mrs Pendle which meant a long walk for which she did not have time.

Then she asked: 'How are you getting on up aloft? Any more revelations, Jeff?' She thought 'Jeff' sounded more friendly than 'Jeffrey' and he had been unable to dissuade her.

He said: 'There's a St Francis.'

'Oh, good. He's always one of the popular saints, isn't he? Because of the animals, I suppose.'

Miles had brought her a series of saints, some perhaps misnamed because his knowledge was not unimpaired, but when he had finished expert opinion would judge who they were. As Jenny was nervous of ladders she had never joined him on the platform. He would have found it intolerable if she had been popping up and down to see for herself.

'Has Adam looked at them lately?' she asked.

Miles said he had not and supposed Jenny would immediately urge her husband to 'take more interest'. Actually Miles was keen to know what King would make of a particular panel but prepared to wait for one of the vicar's polite and diffident requests to be allowed on to the platform.

In his abrupt way Miles handed Jenny his empty mug. He believed, mistakenly, that her eyes were on his back as he mounted the ladder but he felt safer with each step that took him out of reach. As soon as he heard the door close behind her he put down his tools and went to the previous panel he had uncovered. The subject was not one he had anticipated, although when he began his excavation he had been swiftly alerted that there was something different. The plaster was unlike that used on the rest. Miles was convinced that someone had previously exposed the central panel.

He guessed that it had been the first rediscovered because it was the easiest to put a ladder against, the arrangement of columns and pews making it trickier with others. It was also in a position where it got marginally more light. Miles pictured the thrill there must have been when the carving emerged; the decision to uncover the row, starting at the left; and then, after three more had been revealed, the fuss that had led to the restoration being cancelled and the offending panel hidden again.

No one could be upset by the first scenes in the row: St Mark accompanied by a winged lion, St Matthew carrying his carpenter's square and St John bearing his chalice with a serpent rising from it. But revealing St John must have forced reconsideration of the central panel. Miles was confident the original assumption was that it referred to St John the Evangelist to whom the church was dedicated. A fanciful serpent writhed across it. Quite how fanciful would not have been apparent until the one in the chalice in the third panel was compared. Then they would have known. They had a basilisk.

Jeffrey Miles hugged to himself the secret of St John's, the fabulous creature who could destroy with a glance. He stroked his fingertips over its mitre-shaped crest, along the sinuous scaly form and he smiled. A medieval craftsman had released it from the block of stone and Miles had resurrected it.

He was interrupted by the door opening and he moved back to St Francis and resumed picking at plaster that persisted in crevices. 'Good morning, Mr Miles,' a country-woman's voice called up to him. She was in her forties, a mildly scruffy woman whose hair looked as though she was growing out a perm.

'Good morning.' In a tone to discourage her.

Mrs Long, widowed mother of three daughters and stalwart of St John's, was not deterred. 'Found any more treasures up there, have you?'

He took his time before replying: 'One or two.'

'It'll mean more visitors, mind, that's what I say. And more visitors means more titivating.' She had come to clean. He thought this laughable while he was causing dust but the church ladies' response to a messy job was to clean more frequently. Mrs Long came more often than anyone else.

Miles had never got close to her but knew her for the type of woman who always smells of polish and home baking.

She unzipped a plastic holdall containing cleaning rags and polishes. 'Heard the news, have you?' He said nothing and she continued, telling him about the police issuing the description of a man wanted in connection with the Mary Cross case. 'They'll get him now,' she said. 'Somebody must have seen him with her and somebody else must know who he is.'

Miles did not comment and she whisked her duster along pews near the chancel, telling him all the while about the police checkpoints and the posters in Hertfield and the rumours about where the man might be hiding.

To Miles's relief Mrs Long was shortly joined by her eldest daughter, Veronica, a vacuous teenager whose youthful insecurity was underlined by the excessive attention she gave to her appearance. At least, Miles thought, they could talk to each other and leave him alone. Even if he had felt like gossiping with either of them he would not have wanted to do it at full volume the length and breadth of the church.

He expected to suffer them for an hour; then Mrs Long would wipe her hands down her apron, make a remark about being needed in the kitchen and hurry away home. It had happened like that half a dozen times since Miles had come. He closed his mind to the Longs and concentrated on his escape from the vicarage.

There was one ideal place to stay which would cost him nothing and be extremely handy. He could sleep in the church. If he did, it would have to be secret. Rather than offend the Kings he would play a charade of walking towards the bus stop each evening and then doubling back. There were three bus stops: one opposite the vicarage gates which would obviously not do; one on the same road but south of the green; and another at the crossroads on the Harpury road, which curled past Benfield to the west.

He decided to pretend he had found somewhere to stay in Harpury, choosing it because it was far enough away, bigger than any of the other villages up that road and therefore less likely that either of the Kings would discover he was not there. He could set off from St John's through a churchyard gate on to a footpath and follow that along the edge of the wood until it met a lane leading to the crossroads. The junction was known as Ayot crossroads because Ayot St Martin, another of the villages in Benfield parish, lay down a lane on the other side of Harpury road.

He assumed he could get in and out of the church without attracting attention and went on to list the things he would require to be comfortable there. He intended, once the Longs had gone, to inspect the tower.

Veronica had been detailed to clean the brass. 'Oh, Mum! I'll get all mucky. Can't I do the dusting, like you said?'

'No, you do the brass today, love. I'm going to pop in to see Jenny in a few minutes and I don't want to go into the vicarage with that stuff on my hands.'

Veronica grizzled but set about the brass. There was little of it and before her mother returned she had come to an end and was wandering about the church aimlessly. She tried to draw Miles into conversation. 'Don't you mind it up there, all on your own?'

'No.'

'No, I suppose you don't. You wouldn't have stuck it all this time, would you?'

He muttered something she was not intended to hear and she sloped off between the pews and began to read aloud in a childish, irritating way from the memorials. Miles dragged his mind back to the tower.

He had to contrive something to sleep on. Perhaps rows of kneelers? He thought he might manage if it were possible to place them so they did not part whenever he moved. They had been freshly made a few years earlier and looked reasonably comfortable. The snag was that he would have to carry them up to the tower at night and return them each morning. And it would be obvious they were being moved because each bore a different embroidered design and he had no chance of putting them back in their normal positions.

Veronica's voice intruded as she wondered about the riches of the Dornaye family who were commemorated in splendid seventeenth-century style. Fortunately she did not read Latin so Miles had to bear only part of the inscriptions on their memorials. She asked whether he could understand Latin and he said yes, a bit.

'What's all this about then?' She jabbed a figure at gilded lettering.

He guessed she wanted him to go down and talk to her but he was not going to be tricked like that. From memory he summarized the eulogy to the Dornayes. Veronica challenged him over something which did not make sense if they were presumed to have gone up to heaven.

Miles went to the edge of the platform to explain. 'It's a pun,' he said. 'It doesn't work in English.' She frowned and he saw she did not know what a pun was so he hurried on, not bothering to unravel it for her. 'Whoever wrote that Latin verse was making a joke about the Dornayes being buried in a vault beneath the church.'

'Oh.' Veronica's eyes slewed to the door leading to the vault. Then she smiled up. Miles hoped it was at recognition of the memorialist's wit and not a sign that she liked him.

He groped for something to say, her 'oh' not having provided a stepping stone to another remark. Finally he said: 'Are they still around here?'

She was at her most vacant, staring up at him in a manner that made him uncomfortable. 'Who?'

'The Dornaye family.' As she still looked blank he had to add: 'Do any of then live near here these days?'

Veronica shook her head, tinted hair swinging. 'No, they were in history.' She understood she had been staring and collected her wits, lowering her eyes and moving away. In her opinion Jeffrey Miles was very good looking, almost fair enough to be called blond, and she loved his steady grey eyes although it was never easy to get them to look her way. And he always had such interesting things to say, providing she could get him talking. It was a bit of luck, her mother going over to see Jenny, because if she had not he might never have said a word.

Veronica abandoned the Dornayes and went to another feature of St John's, a plaque, conveniently in English, recalling Arthur Bellerman, an eighteenth-century man who had compiled a local flora and endowed a chair at a university. Veronica did not understand what a flora was nor how a chair could be endowed. She was sure Jeffrey Miles would have the answers and might have asked him if she had not felt a trifle foolish at having gazed at him so admiringly. Instead, she chose to wait until she was more composed. But her mother came back before her composure was entirely recovered and Veronica left with her, none the wiser about Arthur Bellerman but elaborating in her imagination her conversation with Miles.

Miles let out his breath in a long sigh that echoed about the nave. Peace again, until the next interruption. He went to the tower, pleased that his memory of the room, with the bell ropes hanging through the ceiling and an embrasure for light, was reliable. The room would do very well.

Then he whiled away a few minutes, noticing the brass Veronica had cleaned and criticizing her for smearing polish on adjoining wood where it would dry to white powder. He looked at the Dornayes, all those Dornayes with their untrustworthy panegyrics and their undeniably fine marble carvings. Re-reading the line that he had confidently announced was a pun he wondered whether he might be wrong, whether the writer had condemned the rich landlord to hell rather than heaven. The mechanism of the church clock stirred ready to strike the hour. He hurried out.

Nobody was in the vicarage kitchen. Miles switched on the radio and listened to the news while he made himself lunch from the salami, tomatoes and brown bread that Jenny had left ready. There was trouble in the Middle East. There was discord in the British Government. There was a takeover battle in the City of London. And then there was an appeal for information about a bearded man wanted for questioning in the Mary Cross case.

Through the window Miles saw Jenny's yellow car pull up in the yard by the back door. He turned off the radio. She waved to him and ran in with a bag in her arms, then back to the car for another. 'Put the kettle on, will you, Jeff?'

He filled the kettle, preparing what to say, how he would say it. She was chattering, telling him she had been to collect the sitting-room curtains from a woman at Ayot St Martin who had made them up for her. The material was a sale bargain from Hertfield and the woman had offered to sew the curtains because Jenny was too busy. 'She's done a fantastic job but there was a fight to get her to take any money. I had to convince her that sewing for the vicarage was not an act of charity like embroidering kneelers for the church.' She tugged open one of the bags to reveal a flowery cotton print. She was still talking. 'I was late calling on her because Mrs Long dropped in. Honestly, Jeff, you don't know how lucky you are hiding in St John's in your eyrie. This place is a madhouse.'

He said it then, when she paused for breath. She gaped, fabric trailing from her hand. '*What* did you say?'

'I'm moving out. I've got somewhere to go so I won't need the room any longer.'

He could not understand why she did not accept it instead of looking at him that silly way with her mouth sagging and her eyes round. As he had no more to say he waited for her to speak.

Jenny swallowed. 'But the carvings. You won't be able to finish them.'

He saw the mistake. 'I'll do the rest of the work. It's just that I won't be living here.'

Relief washed over her. Adam had been impressing on her that Miles was shy and did not welcome her bouncing up to him, but it went against her nature not to be friendly and when he said he was going she was afraid it was because of her. She recovered with a smile. 'Oh, that's all right, then. I was afraid . . . Well, it would be sad if the panels weren't finished.'

The kettle boiled and she switched it off and made tea, asking: 'Where are you going to live?'

'Harpury,' he lied.

'*Harpury*? That's miles away.'

'About seven.' It said so on the signpost at Ayot cross-roads: seven miles north to Harpury and three south to Hertfield. He rapidly invented an exact address in case he was asked for one but he was saved from saying any more

23

because the telephone rang. While she made excuses for the vicar's absence Miles carried his sandwich to his room.

He expected her to join him in as many minutes as it took to get off the telephone and pour the tea. He did not care. This would be her last visit because when he went back to the church after lunch he would take his grey bag and all his possessions with him. He faced an uncomfortable night on the floor of the tower room before buying a sleeping bag in Hertfield next day but it would be worth it to be free. No one was willing to believe he had come to Benfield purely to do a job and not to provide interest for them.

Women were the worst. There had been one at the last place he lived, after leaving hospital, a real nuisance always trailing after him, always bothering him. He had tried asking her politely to leave him alone but she did not take him seriously and in the end he'd had to be brutal. As he stuffed his clothes into the bag he told himself it was not at all the same problem with Jenny. She was happily married, not looking for sex.

3

The photofit picture did not lead to an arrest and Pauline Williams did not ring the police. She had laughed off Marion Knox's assertion that the newspaper picture was of Dale but on Wednesday, when he was away at Brigges's Manchester factory, everyone in the department had seen the television news and the morning papers and arrived with a quip. They indulged in some fanciful talk about his suitability for the role of murderer. He had, according to them, the opportunity and they were willing to speculate about motive. Rather than admit checking on him, Pauline said nothing about his Sheffield visit proving he was nowhere near Hertfield at the time of the crime.

Marion gave her the sort of knowing look Ruth James was apt to give other members of the soap opera cast but they both kept quiet about the letter which, Marion obviously believed, indicated a motive of sorts. Someone started on a second-hand story apparently designed to show Dale as a man ruled by sexual passion but it lost much in the telling and became farcical. Also, there were conflicting accounts and the point was lost. A telephone rang. Pauline went back to her office.

From the morning paper on her desk the face, which was in some respects so like Dale's, looked out at her. The report repeated the police appeal for a man of average build with brown hair and beard who had been seen on the Harpury road late on 17 May. Pauline tossed the paper aside and switched on her word processor. The description fitted thousands of men. Who was she to accuse Roger Dale, especially when he had a perfect alibi? She had inserted a disk and called up a menu before she paused to wonder about the perfection of that alibi.

Dale had written the entry in the desk diary himself and could have done so at any time. She had no recollection of his trip, which might have been because it was routine or else because it happened while she was off sick. She flicked over the pages of her pocket diary until she found a note of her appointment at the doctor's surgery: 15 May. So that was it. She had not been in the office when Dale went to Sheffield. *If* he went. No one else in the department would have been told where he claimed to be. Her absence robbed him of support for his story but also meant she could not deny it if it were untrue.

The police would check with the Sheffield factory if they were interested in Dale. She did not feel justified in doing that. How could she explain to distant colleagues? Or to Dale if he learned of her call? She keyed in a code, entered a file and stopped again.

Her most persuasive reason for not ringing the police up to this point was that Dale could be shown to have been away from the area when the murder was committed. She had now raised a doubt about that. Pauline took up the newspaper, scanning for the telephone number in the appeal for information. But she flopped the paper down, accusing herself of being malicious and meddlesome. He had been through a road check, maybe others he had not mentioned, and the police had been satisfied he was not the man they sought. They had let him go and so must she.

Yet when she had finished editing the file she went to his desk and opened a drawer, foolishly feeling that the framed faces of the Dale children were watching. The manila file she took out contained invoices he would submit with his expenses claim for the money to reimburse him. Expenses were paid every two months and May's invoices would not be presented until the beginning of July.

Pauline found a bill for two nights in a hotel near Sheffield. That was the proof she had been seeking, an irrefutable piece of paper backing up the evidence of the desk diary. Roger Dale had been in Sheffield on 16 and 17 May.

To her shame she was reluctant to accept this and gave way to impulse, promising that after one more check she would let the matter rest. Or call the police.

She telephoned the hotel in Yorkshire. No one called Roger Dale had stayed there.

In Manchester Roger Dale was interviewing a retiring manager, preparing an article on a new production line and generally persuading people at the factory that they got a fair share of attention from their house journal. He was also taking photographs to accompany his articles. His predecessors had not done this but Dale made it sound like enthusiasm and economy and his employers were impressed. Dale had another reason, one he did not expect them to find out.

After the interview he was taken to lunch at an expensive restaurant, to flatter the manager's ego rather than Dale's. They did not return to the factory until mid-afternoon when Dale began work on the article about the production line. Ranks of women in white overalls had been replaced by a couple of robot arms. It was efficient, clean, quiet, depressing and far less photogenic. Dale took a handful of unimaginative shots and then brightened as someone interrupted with a request that he talk to Charmaine Swift who had recently won a holiday camp beauty contest.

Charmaine was blonde and bubbly and three weeks after her holiday her dark roots were showing. Unabashed, she grinned for a decorous photograph for *Pinboard* and told Dale she had set her sights on the beauty queen circuit. He wrote it all down and encouraged her but part of his attention was on a group of girls down the room, one in particular. His job gave him the freedom to go and speak to them. The one in particular was called Sandra Sutton.

By the time he left the factory Sandra Sutton had agreed to meet him that evening. Before then he had other business. He had to call at the printers where what he euphemistically called his photography magazine was printed. Although the printers thought *Angles* increasingly daring they took the money each month and did not comment. Their involvement was slight. Dale brought camera-ready artwork, they printed and if anybody ever questioned the decency or legality of those pages their answer would be that they were too busy to sit around reading the stuff. So far no one had asked.

Dale had a partner in *Angles*, a man called Al Lomax who had put up the money to start it but left the content and production to Dale. It was as 'R. Dales' that an approximation of the editor's name appeared and a clutch of pseudonyms covered his activities as photographer. Under other names he was author of articles giving the reader tips on photography and the magazine its only grounds for claiming to be a serious publication. Certainly the advertisements did nothing to enhance its reputation.

'Bit of a scorcher this time,' remarked a printer who wore a flat cap to cover a bald head.

Dale took this as a compliment. He issued final instructions, corrected a mistake and left the printers to run the magazine during the night for him to collect copies next morning. When he had delivered them to Hertfield Lomax would mail them to subscribers.

Dale was early at the pub to meet Sandra. One day, he supposed, a girl would have second thoughts and not turn up. But he reckoned he could pick the right ones. Not the Charmaines with their contrived modesty and their airy-fairy ambitions about being Miss World. More the Sandra Suttons, the ones who looked able and willing. Especially willing.

Sandra came. She had spent a lot of time on her make-up and her hair was freshly washed and curled. At the factory she had worn a white overall as they all had. Only Charmaine had taken hers off and not until she was clear of a clean area. Now Sandra wore high-heeled sandals, cheap fashionable clothes in a sophisticated style and a cascade of gold chains against the creamy skin of her throat. She looked exactly like a teenager dressing up as a mature woman.

He bought her a drink. She asked for a complicated cocktail which she had probably never heard of apart from on television. He said the pub did not do that kind of thing and fetched her a Martini.

'About the modelling,' she began, in a strong Manchester accent, after her first sip.

28

'Well, not here,' he said laughing at her.

She sipped again and said: 'I mean, I haven't heard of your agency or anything.'

'You won't,' he said smoothly. 'We never advertise. It's not necessary because we specialize in spotting new talent and sending the girls' pictures to the magazines.'

Her eyes narrowed. 'But I won't have to pay you for the pictures? You did say that, didn't you?'

'Not a penny. We get paid by the magazines so there's no reason to charge you, is there?' He picked up a menu from the table beside them. Off the bar was a small dining room. 'I thought we'd eat here.'

She agreed, a shade downcast having hoped for somewhere grander. The pub was hardly worth the effort of dressing up and afterwards . . . Well, she would wait and see.

Afterwards Dale drove her to his hotel. She was in luck, he thought. Sometimes he stayed in rundown places and the girls hardly had space to pose. Sandra Sutton was getting star treatment: a double room because that was all the hotel had spare when he booked. He closed the curtains and opened a bottle of wine from his briefcase. She was terribly impressed with that. She preened at the long wardrobe mirror while he poured wine into a pair of thick glass tumblers from the bathroom.

Sandra knew better than to drink it. She had accepted the Martini and bluffed her way through wine at supper. Now she took the tiniest taste and set the glass down on a bedside table. 'We can't have me looking cross-eyed at the camera, can we?' she joked. And waited for him to tell her what he wanted her to do.

Dale did not share her reluctance about the wine. He drank a glass before answering, his eyes crawling over her while she assumed he was assessing light, considering angles, noting her finer points. Sandra Sutton did not have finer points. But she was willing.

She was dumpy with a retroussé nose. But straight on the line of the nose did not show and her skin was perfection and her blondeness the genuine unadulterated thing.

And then he had to get the camera out and make authoritative suggestions about where she stood and how she looked. She obliged. She was biddable. Oh yes, he could always pick them.

It was no good choosing someone who had a brain or religion or an overdose of modesty. The girl had to be ready. She must have previously thought of it for herself so that his proposal that she become a model was only confirmation of her self-assessment.

First they did the fashion poses, Sandra trying to appear slinky as her flesh strained against the seams of her skirt. Then they did some casual shots, where her blouse buttons had come undone and her skirt had ridden up her thighs. Eventually there was just Sandra and her gold chains.

Dale never had to suggest that. He always waited for it to come from them and it always did. Like he said, he could pick them.

'I ought to have put make-up on that,' said Sandra cutting through his concentration.

He lowered the camera. 'What?'

'My appendix scar. It's not very neat but I'm sure make-up would hide it.'

The scar was a vivid slash. He said it was nothing to worry about. He made her turn this way and that, liking the glow of her rich young skin in lamplight and ignoring the imprint on her flesh of the brassière she was outgrowing.

He was running out of ideas. Just a few more poses to go and in that time he had to make up his mind what else to risk with her. Sandra had thoughts of her own, wanting to play with the wardrobe mirror so there would be two images of her, front and reflected rear or vice versa. He did not explain that without proper lighting it would be disastrous and that the last thing he required was a photograph of himself pointing the camera at a naked seventeen-year-old in a hotel bedroom. He pointed the camera.

Sandra preferred her poses to some of his. She did not go for that kittenish stuff where she curled on pillows or those where she looked as though she expected to be spanked. She liked to wear her high, high-heeled sandals so her breasts tipped forward and her legs were elongated, slimmer.

Dale asked her to move her head, hoping her face would look less immature, but she could not see what he wanted. He went to her, taking her jaw in his hand and gently swivelling. Her baby-blue eyes met his with a gleam of collusion. He kissed her, a palm cradling her breast. The time had come to forget about the camera and have sex with her, the only question being whether she stayed all night or expected a taxi later.

She demurred, pulling away from him with a laugh. 'If we did *that* I'd think you weren't serious about the modelling.'

He protested mildly and took a few more shots. And then he tried again but Sandra ducked into the bathroom and dragged on her clothes. Two minutes later she was dressed and ready to leave. She was friendly and unruffled but definitely not getting into bed with him. She *said* nothing but he understood she regarded it as a game she had just won. She talked instead about modelling and asked how soon she could have prints of the photographs.

'I think I ought to have approval,' she said. He raised a quizzical eyebrow as he refilled his tumbler. She explained: 'Of the photographs. I mean, I don't want you to send the magazines any pictures I don't like. After all, it's my career we're talking about, isn't it?

He promised to post prints to her in the next few days and then rang for a taxi and sent her home. After she had gone he walked restlessly about the room, annoyed that he had been unable to persuade her to stay although it was risky with girls who worked for Brigges. He could not slip into a pseudonym and if he grew too determined they might scream blue murder all the way to London and *Pinboard* would be looking for a new editor. Worse, they might go to the police. He had to avoid that. He had lost control once and the result had been disastrous. Oh yes, it was risky. And oh yes, he enjoyed the risk.

Dale ran a bath, tipped the rest of the wine down the washbasin, rinsed lipstick from the glass Sandra had touched, straightened the bed and put away his camera. He forgot about her. He bathed, watched television, turned the sound down and telephoned Sheila to say he had been working all evening and just reached the hotel. She sympathized as she always did when she heard this tale. He interrupted to ask after Caroline and Timothy. They were fine, she said, except that they were upset about Rusty and the spaceman was still missing.

'Why should they care about Rusty? He growls at them through the fence,' Dale said, his eyes on the screen.

'I know, but Mrs Catesby told them he's been stolen. She's been to the police and they more or less said they're too busy looking for Mary Cross's killer to chase around after a dog which has run off. So she came to me in tears.'

Dale said it was a lot of fuss about a feeble old pet and he did not see why his children should get upset about it.

Sheila said: 'Well, obviously they think it would be terrible to be taken away from your home and your family . . .'

'Mrs Catesby's hardly Rusty's mother!' But that was not the point. The point was that Sheila had upset the children again. He was afraid they were going to grow up as nervous as she was. Dale blamed her over-protective parents for his wife's inability to keep a sense of proportion and he had fended them off so their visits to Harpury were rare and their influence on his children minimal although they telephoned Sheila frequently.

When he came off the line he had another of those spells when he wondered how he had come to marry her and how much longer it could last. The answer to one of the questions was Caroline. And the answer to the other was that Sheila could not cope without him and it was unthinkable to let his children take the consequences of being left with her while she slid into neurosis.

Besides, at present *he* needed *her*. She did not know and could never be told but her fragile state was useful to him. If the need arose she would be as compliant about saying what he wanted as Sandra Sutton had been about posing the way he liked.

The need might have arisen that very day but Pauline Williams was cultivating guilt about her own conduct instead of picking up the telephone and calling the police.

4

Miles stood in the fading light of St John's on Wednesday and waited for the noise to start up again. But Stan Albury, who did a variety of jobs for church and vicarage, had finished mowing between the graves. The old man rumbled the petrol mower towards a shed in the vicarage garden.

The vicar and Jenny were both out and it had not been necessary for Miles to pretend he was catching a bus to Harpury. Albury had not seen him, either. Miles went into the vestry.

There was an oak chest there, nothing special but with an ornate lock. That did not matter because most of the church keys were kept in the vestry. Miles picked up one with a tag which read 'chest'. He remembered a remark made by King when he was shown around the church weeks ago. 'No copes in that, just a moth-eaten old rug.'

The lid made a rasping sound as Miles lifted it. In the chest's darkness was a rug, a kelim, not heavy but big enough to cover the vestry floor. Probably it had lain there until somebody donated the wall-to-wall carpet that kept feet off cold stones. He locked the chest, slung the rug over his shoulder and carried it into the tower.

The bell loft was not spacious. It had nothing to recommend it except privacy. Bell-ringing practice was once a month and would not come round again for three weeks. As long as Miles removed his things before Saturday weddings, Sunday services and bell-ringing practice his nights in the loft would be secret.

He spread the rug and then folded it to form a pad to lie on. With his spare clothing over him for warmth and a kneeler from a pew as a pillow he could manage for one night before buying a sleeping bag. Miles started down the tower stairs.

As he reached the foot he heard voices in the porch and the heavy door swung. Then there was the snap of a light switch and Miles saw Jenny with a man he did not recognize.

They appeared very friendly and Jenny was saying, as she led him to the aisle: 'It's going to be absolutely wonderful. There!'

The man made enthusiastic murmurs. Then: 'Let's go up.'

'Not me, Don, but you go if you like.'

He did, climbing to the platform and calling down: 'They're fantastic, Jenny. I told you they would be. You're lucky they weren't smashed at the time of the Reformation but simply covered up.'

He walked along the platform admiring the carvings but not, Miles noted, in a particularly informed way. When he got to the basilisk he just laughed and said: 'Only a medieval mind could conjure up this one. Why do you suppose they put such a hideous snake here?'

'The serpent's the symbol of St John the Evangelist,' Jenny explained. 'But never mind that ugly thing. Look at the St Francis, the one Jeff's working on. That's my favourite so far.'

The man said he hoped to have time to see them again next day. 'I'd like to meet our Jeffrey Miles and hear what he has to say about these things.'

Jenny protected Miles. 'You won't be welcome, Don. I find it impossible to draw him out of his shell. Adam says he's a loner and I ought to keep away, but how does Adam know? I'm sure Jeff's just terribly shy.'

The man smiled affectionately. 'Perhaps the breakthrough will come tomorrow when I meet him.'

When he was back on ground level Jenny begged him not to trouble Miles. 'Look, Don, I almost scared him away by showing too much interest and if he goes the job won't get finished. Adam and I have to be so careful not to upset him. We have to come creeping in here in the evenings like a couple of church robbers to see what he's found.'

She related how Miles had moved out of the vicarage and said she was worried about him. 'He was obviously happy when he came here. Quiet, of course, but he seemed content. Then all of a sudden he was off, with no explanation.'

The man sympathized. 'And you can't ask because he'll treat it as an intrusion? Poor Jenny. It sounds as though you've got a lame duck who refuses your help . . .'

They turned off the light and went out, their voices diminishing across the churchyard. Miles seethed in the sudden blackness. So! The polite Reverend Adam King had been sneaking around, checking up on him, wanting to see whether the work was being done fast enough to give value for his money no doubt! Any time of evening the vicar or his wife and their friends might come snooping, climbing his ladder, prowling about wherever the fancy took them.

Abruptly Miles went back to the bell loft where he snatched up the rug and his bag. Too angry to care about making a noise, he let them buffet the walls as he descended. Then he flung them on the floor in the nave. He dropped the rug back in the chest and then grabbed the bag and let himself out into the churchyard.

It would serve the Kings right if he just disappeared, he thought, and let them practise their deceit on somebody else. If he went they would have to find another man to take on the work and that would not be easy. They did not realize how lucky they were to have someone with experience of working with old stone and willing to give the time. They might never find anyone else and they would have to stop showing off about how they had discovered the carvings.

Miles stamped away between the gravestones, heading for the gate to the path beside the wood, the route to the bus stop. Leaving like this, he thought, he would not have to endure any longer the Kings' possessiveness about the carvings. They were *his*, not theirs. They had done nothing for them. And now, because of their underhand ways, nobody would have them.

But, of course, Miles himself had to have them. Whatever the Kings had done, he could not walk off into the night and abandon his carvings. His feelings about the stones had reached a peak of feverish intensity. When he sat alone with them his spirit was changed. With joy he shared in the triumph of their distant creator. His tools followed where the medieval craftsman's chisels had been. Folds of garments, faces of saints, curlicues and creatures grew beneath his hands as they had beneath the ancient mason's. Their achievements were indistinguishable. More, there were times when Miles felt the presence of that creator within him, when his hands seemed guided and his anticipation of what lay under the shroud of plaster was acute and accurate.

He did not actually reason that he would have to stay, that the carvings would not free him. But he left the footpath and turned into the wood, keeping clear of paths. The evening was dry and warm, it would do him no harm to sleep out of doors for a night. He pressed on into the deepest cover, opened his bag, took out his waterproof nylon jacket and spread it as a ground sheet.

Birdsong. A squirrel on a tree trunk. Furtive movements of timorous creatures. Miles lay still, eyes open, mind uncomprehending until the events of Wednesday evening flooded his brain and he remembered where he was and why. He sat up, sending the squirrel scudding away. The wood was beautiful. Early light gave colours a delicacy they would lose as the day grew older.

The church clock struck telling him the time. He got to his feet, not too stiff. He felt calm, protected. He had not woken once during the night, unlike that first time he ever slept out. Miles checked himself. There was no use thinking about it. But the memory had been disturbed and he was compelled to remember. He was a child, sleeping out for the thrill of it in a neighbour's shrubbery. His friend went snivelling home before it was even truly dark but Miles was braver. He liked it there alone. But then the great dog came snuffling through the rhododendrons and found him. He could not go home because his family did not know he was out of the house and so he stayed, waking fearfully at every night-time noise in case the lolloping animal was coming back.

Next morning he could not help telling them, or some of it at least. 'Nonsense,' they said. 'Who in the village owns a dog like that? And why ever were you trespassing among Mr

Tanner's rhododendrons?' And because they did not believe him about the dog he never told them about the man who came after it, the man who sat down to talk and put his hands on Miles and took away his will so that he did not resist the touching.

He had not had an unhappy childhood although he was the quiet one in a big family, a middle child whose older brother and sisters were clever and whose younger ones were boisterous. When the rest were disappointed that the house in Surrey had to be given up and they had to leave the setting and the people they had known all their lives, Miles looked forward to the relative anonymity of a fresh place. The fresh place was a seaside town on the south coast, a place of long, lonely cliff walks and unpeopled views. He used to fantasize about taking one of the boats from a creek and sailing away but he never did it, he always walked home to the noisy house.

Gregarious themselves, his family teased him for his solitude and accused him of being moody. But the black moods did not begin until later and by then he had escaped his family. First there was college, although he did not stay long. Then there were jobs, a series of them, each more isolating than the last. The best was with Mr Withers, a mason cleaning and restoring church stonework. If the old man had not died of influenza while Miles was in hospital, he would have gone back to him. Instead he was cut adrift until he was told about Benfield.

Tentatively the squirrel returned and watched Miles pack his bag and carry it away to St John's. Miles was wishing he understood the bus timetables better so he could have gone to Hertfield, arranged somewhere to stay and returned in time to begin work. He considered walking to the bus stop south of the green where a timetable was displayed but that would put him in full view of most of the population of Benfield when he was meant to be travelling from Harpury. He knew there was no timetable at Ayot crossroads because once when he walked by a woman asked him how long she would have to wait for a ride.

He entered the church and began delicately prising the

plaster from intricate animals around St Francis, interrupted only once when Jenny brought coffee and asked brightly: 'How was the journey from Harpury, Jeff?' He said he had not had any problems.

Jenny could not stay and talk because one of her women's groups was meeting at the vicarage. She excused herself and hurried away. Miles sat in the porch facing the wood. Birds darted from its depths, sunlight colouring their forms. The sky was cerulean and fields towards Ayot St Martin shimmered. Miles turned his mind to the search he must make in Hertfield that evening for somewhere cheap to stay. Harpury was too far off to be used outside a fiction.

Jenny was in her kitchen when he called at lunchtime. She had made a substantial soup with hunks of vegetables, a filling dish whose aroma drew him as soon as he opened the door. He was famished but only then realized he had eaten nothing since lunch on Wednesday. He accepted a second bowl of soup and another bread roll, and it was because of this that he was there when the police inspector came.

Miles had met Inspector Addison once or twice before because the man lived at Ayot St Martin. When Mary Cross's body was found Addison had been among the officers going from house to house asking questions. He had called at the vicarage then and that was how it had come out that Jenny had seen a girl who might have been Mary. Jenny had also answered for the men in her house: her husband had been at a meeting in Hertfield until late on 17 May and Miles had been in the vicarage all evening with her.

Miles was grateful to her on that occasion. He had not relished nosiness from the police and Jenny's information meant he was spared more than the most cursory of inquiries. So why had Addison come back? Neither Miles nor the vicar was bearded and the police were seeking a bearded man.

Addison, a solid, square-jawed countryman, said he was on his way home to lunch but a cup of tea would be welcome. Before she poured it Jenny fetched a magazine and showed it to him. He browsed until the tea was set in front of him. Then he said: 'Not very pleasant, I agree, Jenny.'

Jenny handed tea to Miles and explained, for his benefit as she had already told Addison on the telephone when she asked him to call: 'It arrived through the post unsolicited at a cottage in the village. The woman who lives there found it in the hands of one of her children and brought it to me because she didn't know what to do about it.'

Addison said: 'Personally I doubt if the magazine is beyond the borders of legality but if it arrived at the house in the way the woman says the publishers ought to be warned off that sort of thing.'

'There aren't any men in the house,' said Jenny. 'It can't have been an embarrassed husband or son lying to her.'

While they talked Addison put the magazine aside. Miles took it up and slowly turned the pages. The magazine was full of pictures of girls with captions stating what photographic equipment had been used. Some pages were text offering advice on photography but clearly the main purpose was to publish pictures of girls. There was no artistry. The girls were not made to look beautiful. The photography was mediocre.

Miles became aware that the other two had finished speaking and were watching him. He passed the magazine to Addison with no comment except that it was time he got back to work. But he did not go straight there. He walked as far as the green and bought things at the village shop.

Addison, meanwhile, was offering to call on Mrs Long. Jenny urged him not to as the woman had been upset to find Veronica reading the magazine and had sought Jenny's advice precisely because she could not face talking to the police about such a thing. Jenny said: 'I wondered whether you might already know about it as it's published in Hertfield.'

But Addison said it had never come to his notice before. He rolled the magazine in his hand and got up to leave. He did not mean to be late home, he said, but he wanted to squeeze time to look at the carvings before leaving St John's. Jenny might have accompanied him but the telephone rang and he saw himself out.

When she came off the line she ran water into a bowl to

wash up the lunch dishes, thinking that whatever the legal position might be the publication was in very poor taste. Maybe Veronica Long was tough enough not to be affected by it when she picked it up off the doormat but Jenny thought it unfortunate it had got into Jeffrey Miles's hands. She had not cared for the rapt way in which he had pored over the pictures. Most men discovering they were being watched studying such a thing would have laughed it off, whatever their private responses, but Miles had not.

Addison was still in the church. He was there when Miles came with his shopping and he caught the split-second objection on the young man's face. 'I daren't climb up there, Jeffrey,' Addison said in a friendly tone to put him at ease. 'I've just been standing here, straining to see up and thinking what a marvellous job you've got.'

Miles said briefly that he was enjoying it. He did not dislike Addison, the man seemed to know how far he should go with people. 'I've found a St Francis,' Miles added after a pause. He was happy to describe it although he did not invite Addison to mount the ladder and see for himself. Showing St Francis or any of the other saints would have done no harm but one day he might invite someone who identified the basilisk and then all the carvings might be covered over again. Miles felt sick at the prospect. If he let that happen he would have broken faith with their creator and something in himself would be destroyed.

Addison gazed up at the panels as Miles talked about them. Then they wandered to the door together, Addison stretching the conversation and tapping rhythmically on the church visitors' book with the rolled magazine until he was ready to leave.

Miles worked calmly through the afternoon, perfecting the St Francis panel. Then he brought his bag down from the platform, added his lunchtime shopping to its contents and went out into the graveyard. He saw no one as he crossed to the far gate and joined the footpath beside the trees, intending to catch the Hertfield bus. But when he reached the stile to the lane he did not use it. For the second night he turned into the wood.

5

Al Lomax was on the telephone when Jenny King marched into the terrace house in Hertfield where the photographic magazine was published. Lomax was making a cryptic call and finding it difficult to know whether the man was truly misunderstanding him or pretending because he had someone with him. Lomax gave up and rang off when Jenny appeared.

He recognized her type: a bossy young middle-class feminist come to tell him his magazine was filth. Lomax had heard it before. He did not bother with a smile. 'What do you want?'

Jenny tried a smile. She recognized his type: rough around the edges, a dirty-minded man acting out his fantasies with young models who thought he was offering them the world. She said: 'You, if you're the editor of *Angles*.'

'Oh, yes? And what do you want the editor for?' Sarcastic now, making her spell it out. In a minute she would be using words like pornography and exploitation.

'I'd like to discuss your methods of promotion because your magazine has fallen into the hands of an impressionable young girl whose mother is very upset about it.'

'Because she didn't get to read it first?' Lomax sneered at her with a poor joke.

Jenny did not flinch. Sounding more priggish than she liked, she said it was reprehensible that such material, plainly intended for male readers, should be pushed through a village letter box where young girls lived. And she was ready to go on but Lomax interrupted: 'Now, come on, lady. This magazine is sent to subscribers. How could it get itself through a letter box in . . . Where did you say it was?'

'Benfield.'

'Yes, Benfield. Well, I'll tell you. It couldn't. We don't need the promotion so why would we do a stupid thing like that? It's an adult magazine.'

They argued about the truth of her story because Lomax was inclined to the opinion that she had made it up as an excuse to burst into his office with a lot of feminist nonsense. She defended herself. He called her a name or two. She said she was neither of those, she was the wife of the vicar of Benfield.

Jenny did not know why she fell back on that. This business was nothing to do with Adam and if he had known her intention he would have urged her not to storm the *Angles* office. But once Inspector Addison had given the impression there were unlikely to be grounds for prosecution she felt that if she did not complain to the editor no one would, and copies would be tumbling through letter boxes all over the country as freely as soap-powder coupons.

Being a vicar's wife was no defence against Lomax. He found fresh ammunition and blasphemed his way through another attack on her. She saw no purpose in going on and left with a threat: 'You haven't heard the last of this, Mr Dales.'

Lomax subsided with laughter as the door banged behind her. She had got the wrong man, never cottoned on that he was not the editor! He planned to have some fun with Roger Dale over this! Then he sobered up and opened a copy of the latest issue, which Dale had delivered from the printers the previous day. Lomax was in the office to address copies to subscribers. He had taken time away from his business to do it and had not bothered to look through the issue until then.

When he finished reading his pudgy face was grim. He went to the window and scowled over the top of the flowery half curtain into the main street. The vicar's lady was being hysterical, of course. No doubt about it. But he reckoned *Angles* had just taken another step in the direction of a courtroom.

Leaving Lomax Jenny called at the greengrocer's shop next door. She bought a pound of tomatoes and asked several questions. That was how she discovered she had not been rowing with R. Dales, the editor, but with Al Lomax who ran a back-street engineering business and 'sometimes gave a hand' at *Angles*.

She felt annoyed at being goaded into argument with a man who was not Dales anyway. The High Street address was the only one she had and she could not keep barging in there in the hope of catching the editor so she would have to try something else. Jenny went to the public library.

First she looked in telephone directories but there was no R. Dales listed although there was an R. Dale at Harpury. She tried various other records but could not find the name with a final 's'. Eventually she made a note of the address of the Harpury Dale with little faith that he would turn out to be the editor. An editor would be certain to publish his name correctly in his own magazine.

As she was replacing the books she was taken aback to see Jeffrey Miles at a table. He was rising. She shoved the rest of the books on the shelves and hurried after him with the offer of a lift to Benfield. But the doors were swinging and he was in the street ahead of her.

Jenny scanned the pavements. Hertfield was busy on Fridays and it had been easy for her to lose him. She kept an eye open for Miles as she hurried to the car park, anxious about time because she wanted to make a call before going to the vicarage but must not be late home as Friday was the day Adam wrote his sermon. That meant he was not to be disturbed by telephone calls or visitors. He was taking a service that morning, which was why Miles was away from St John's, but by afternoon would want to shut himself in his study.

And then she spotted Miles. Her pace quickened. When she lost him once more she still did not understand that her appearance had sent him dodging into shops and hanging about in alleys. She reached her car and took the road north.

Her natural curiosity would not let her forget Miles. She was intrigued to know who had lured him to Harpury. He had never mentioned friends. One other thing puzzled her: she did not see how the arrangement to live there had been made. All the while he had been at the vicarage he had received no letters and not used the telephone. She did not like to believe he had used the telephone kiosk on the green rather than risk being overheard at the vicarage but admitted the possibility.

She wished she had learned more about Miles when her cousin, who had pressed Adam to open up the carvings and had found Miles for him, had stayed overnight at Benfield on Wednesday. But Don had been more enthusiastic about discussing the carvings than the young man working on them.

Her thoughts were deflected as she passed the place where Mary Cross's battered body had been found. Long after the checkpoints and the posters had gone that stretch of road would bring the savagery back to mind.

She overtook the Harpury bus. Jeffrey Miles, her thoughts ran, said he was living at Harpury but instead of staying there on the day he was starting work late he had travelled to Hertfield. There was sure to be a better library there than in Harpury and she knew he was a keen reader: he had spent most of his evenings at the vicarage in his room with a book. But for all that, Jenny could not rid herself of the suspicion that Miles had lied about moving to Harpury.

She turned east to the junction where she had once seen a neatly dressed teenager who might have been Mary Cross. Normally Jenny would have gone home by the road which passed the village green but as she was making a detour to visit Mrs Pendle it was quicker to use the Harpury road and cut through to Back Lane where the old woman lived.

Ada Pendle was not particularly old but increasingly infirm. She and Jenny had taken to each other as soon as Jenny and Adam arrived in Benfield although the local women spoke about Mrs Pendle with such deference that Jenny was nervous when she made her first call.

Mrs Pendle's independence impressed them because her nearest neighbours were weekenders who would be of no use to her in a weekday emergency. Jenny was a considerable help to her, making regular visits interspersed with telephone calls.

The few Benfield people who had resisted Jenny's energetic approach to life when she had first burst upon them had been won round. The vicar's wife was as good as her word, not only willing to serve the community but vigorously doing so. She had an advantage over Adam who, in their first months at St John's, heard repeated murmurs about the way his predecessor had done things. Jenny had no predecessor in recent memory because the previous incumbent had been an aged bachelor.

She unlatched the gate at Pendle Cottage and went into a front garden of spring flowers. The gate was broken. A heavy strut which had gradually lost its nails had finally dropped off and lay by the hedge. Jenny made a mental note to bring a hammer and nails with her next time and tap it back into position. She rattled the letter box and called out as she let herself in.

Mrs Pendle's voice came from the sitting room at the back of the house. 'Come in, Jenny.'

Soon after she moved into the cottage in her sixties Mrs Pendle changed its name to her own, a practical measure to help the postman and prevent letters slipping by mistake through other cottage doors in the lane. Absentee neighbours had always been a slight nuisance.

'How are you, Mrs Pendle?' Jenny had not reached the 'Ada' stage but expected it was not far off.

Mrs Pendle looked frail, her fine papery skin unhealthily yellow. She was not a woman to complain, especially when grumbling might cause unhappiness which had nothing to do with her arthritis. She pulled a wry face. 'Last night wasn't one of my best.' She had been awake in considerable pain.

'You've got enough tablets, haven't you?' Jenny had fetched her a prescription not long ago.

Mrs Pendle waved a hand at a chair. 'Hundreds. Plenty. Sit down and tell me what's happening in the outside world. That's what I require, something to arouse my interest beyond my own four walls.'

They talked for a while but Jenny was aware that Mrs Pendle was not pulling her weight in the conversation. Despite her brave words she was not at all well. She tensed her body and her eyes were half shut against pain. But when Jenny glanced furtively at her watch Mrs Pendle was alert enough to notice. 'Don't apologize,' she said. 'You get back to the vicarage and look after your husband. I know where your duties lie, my dear. Off you go, but come and see me again soon.'

She did not stir from her armchair. Jenny was concerned about that. In winter or when it was cold and damp Mrs Pendle did not come out but the weather had been hot and dry, too dry, for weeks and yet she could not manage the effort of waving her off up the lane.

Jenny extracted a final promise that Mrs Pendle would telephone if she wanted help or company. 'And don't you worry about my duties at the vicarage,' she said lightly. 'I've got the whole of Benfield at my beck and call.' They both laughed because it was true.

When her telephone rang later she realized it was serious. Mrs Pendle would never have troubled her otherwise. Before she set out for the cottage again Jenny called Dr Bourton.

Neither she nor her husband noticed that Jeffrey Miles did not turn up for work that day. The Reverend Adam King was struggling with his Sunday text and his wife had too many other concerns to spare another thought for Miles and his unexpected presence in Hertfield.

6

Al Lomax spent Friday afternoon sealing copies of *Angles* in brown envelopes and addressing them to subscribers. It was a tedious time-consuming job but he had agreed to be responsible for it. Roger Dale did virtually everything else.

Lomax expected Dale to call at the office and he wanted to talk to him, not only about the things Dale expected him to mention but also about the slide in the standard of *Angles*. He meant to start with the quality of the pictures. There had been no hint when they launched the publication three years earlier that Dale planned to take the pictures. If there had been Lomax would have objected, loudly. Dale was adequate for the type of photographs he took for his house magazine: firing squad poses of groups of staff or pointing pictures where someone indicated how high the flood water had been in the canteen. Glamour was different. You had to be a bit artistic for that. And *Angles* had become plain crude.

It would not be the first time he had called a halt to Dale's fun. Dale's advertisements had caused the trouble before. Lomax had stumbled across a batch of replies from youngsters looking for modelling work and from others who thought something less legal was required. Dale defended his practice of slipping his own advertisements among the small ads. He said *Angles* needed cheap models and the wording did not identify the magazine. But Lomax had the last word: if Dale wanted to run those advertisements he was not to use the magazine's address because that was Lomax's property.

Roger Dale arrived in Hertfield about 4 p.m. He had fixed an early interview with a man in north London and let Pauline Williams believe it would last all afternoon. He was normally able to organize things in such a way that he took time off for *Angles* whenever he chose but on this day was especially glad to get out of the office. Ralph Gough and his press office staff had been making jokes about Dale's likeness to the photofit picture, and Pauline had been in a funny mood, avoiding talking to him. He thought it a great shame he had failed to have her shifted out of his office. She had never been decorative and now she was sullen.

He could have reached Hertfield even sooner but he had contrived a route to avoid checkpoints and it worked. When he breezed into the *Angles* office he was feeling self congratulatory. Then he saw Lomax's face.

'What's the matter, Al?' His first thought was that the police had been there. Lomax was not packing the copies. He was by the window and the subscribers' list was on the desk. Lomax did not look at him. Dale noticed how the sun through Lomax's reddish hair showed how thin it had become. In a very few years, at forty, he would have a bald pate.

Lomax said: '*Angles*, Roger. That's what's wrong.'

Dale had heard the tone before. Quiet. Very flat. Rather menacing. He could guess why but was not going to admit it. He said: 'I think it looks pretty good and I got it away from the printers on time. One of the smoothest runs we've had.'

'We're going to have a smooth run straight into the dock at St Albans Crown Court the way you're going on.' Lomax had forgotten about building up to it carefully by first attacking the quality of the pictures.

Dale picked up a copy from the desk. He laughed derisively as he flicked over the pages. Lomax turned. 'I mean it, Roger. You've overstepped the mark. And not once. I've been looking through some back numbers this after-noon . . .'

Dale was astonished Lomax had not pored eagerly over the magazine each time it appeared. He kept his astonishment to himself and said: 'There've never been any complaints.'

'You're getting one now,' said Lomax evenly.

Dale protested but Lomax raised his voice and said: 'Understand this, Roger. You clean up *Angles* or I get out. Find a decent photographer and tone things down. And get some older models. Some of those kids look as though they're below the age of consent.'

Dale tried again but Lomax cut in: 'I don't want to know where you've been finding them. That's your business. Mine's to keep my name out of anything that's running unnecessary risks with the law.'

Dale made a gesture of acquiescence and chucked the magazine back on the desk. He could not understand why Lomax had picked this moment to create a fuss. Everything had been fine when they had spoken on the telephone early that morning. Lomax had only been interested in the size of the printers' bill and the amount of profit the issue would make. Oh, and he had been worried about the length of time he was having to spend away from his business. Something had happened causing him to take a jaundiced view of their little money spinner.

Dale expected the explanation to emerge in due course and did not prod. He preferred to switch to a different topic, the one he had been looking forward to all day. Dogs. He asked Lomax if there was any news about the dogs.

Lomax said he had telephoned the man but it had been inconclusive. He tried again right away and held another cryptic conversation after which he said to Dale: 'It's on. Sunday. You're all right if you come with me.'

Dale felt a flush of excitement. He had never been to a dog fight. Lomax went to them, he had discovered that much, but it was an illegal and clandestine sport and Dale had been angling for an invitation for months.

Lomax said: 'We'll meet here on Sunday morning and I'll take you over there.'

'Where will it be, roughly?' Dale was thinking about the lie he would have to tell at home to give himself freedom. Was it to be a lie to cover a couple of hours? Or longer?

Lomax grinned. 'Who knows? We'll meet the boys on Sunday, then we'll know.'

Dale was slyly amused by the inconsistency of Lomax flapping about the risks attached to *Angles* while getting deeper into something which was unquestionably illegal. He had a criminal record, although he had kept out of trouble for a long time, and claimed he was anxious to avoid any more court appearances. That was the only bit of it Dale could understand.

The telephone rang and Lomax held another of his discussions which were largely unintelligible to an over-hearer. The part that came through to Dale was that a man was offering Lomax a share in an American pit terrier, a type bred especially for the ring.

What he did not know was how expensive that sort of dog was and that if he bought it Lomax would have to sell his interest in *Angles*. Unaware, and feeling that the moment of Lomax's wrath had passed, Dale went into the darkroom and made some prints of the Sandra Sutton photographs. When he emerged Lomax was methodically packing the subscribers' copies.

Suddenly Lomax said: 'I had a visitor today, Roger.' And told him about Jenny King. He wanted Dale's assurance that there had been no mailshots or any other way in which the magazine could have landed on a woman's doormat in Benfield. Dale was adamant. He whisked up the subscribers' list but Lomax had already checked that no one in the area bought *Angles*.

'Mrs King looks set to make an almighty fuss,' said Lomax. 'I reckon you ought to use your smoothest manner and go and talk her out of it, don't you?'

Dale did not want to but would have agreed to almost anything to placate Al Lomax rather than find his invitation to the dog fight cancelled. He gave his partner a leering smile and said he was pretty good at smooth talking women.

Dale was irritated to meet another checkpoint as he headed for Benfield. He had suspected he might but could not afford to offer Lomax that as an excuse for not calling at the vicarage. Lomax would have wanted to know why he was nervous about policemen.

Prepared, Dale had taken precautions. The prints of Sandra Sutton were in the darkroom at the *Angles* office. There was no copy of the magazine in his car, far less the pages of artwork he had carried when stopped at the beginning of the week. The police could poke around in the boot for as long as they liked. He would ask them to look out for a plastic spaceman.

But the police did not inspect the boot. They wanted to know where he was going and where he had been. A sergeant said: 'You know this area pretty well, do you, sir?'

Dale kept a grip on his feelings and said: 'Fairly well.' It had been a slip to elaborate about the route he was going to take. He should have left off at the vicarage but when they asked where he would go next he explained he intended to take lanes to bring him to the Harpury road at a junction south of Ayot crossroads. Signposting was sparse. A man would have to know those lanes before he could use them with confidence. And that junction was the one where the vicar's wife claimed she had seen Mary Cross.

The police asked more questions and Dale pictured the scene in their computer room when they compared the new information with the old. 'He'd said he drove from Harpury to London via Hertfield and left home early to avoid heavy traffic; but we stopped him much later one morning and then he said he sometimes broke the morning run at Hertfield. He'd said he left his London office at 6 p.m. and took the same route back; but we caught him in the area at other times of evening and on other roads. Everything he said at first, he qualified later.'

Dale felt weak as he wondered how long it would be before one of them announced that he was the only man who matched the description they had issued and could have been in the area on 17 May. It would take little time to find out he had lied about Sheffield. They could not rapidly check everything they were told by every driver they stopped, but as his name recurred and doubts mounted it would be a simple step to send a detective to check a hotel register and show the receptionist the photofit picture.

When the police at the checkpoint let him go Dale continued to Benfield, switching his mind from Mary Cross to Jenny King. He was rehearsing what to say, preparing to be disarming and penitent in whatever proportions were required. Mrs King must not be allowed to go to the police with her quibbles about *Angles*.

51

Dale had a fair idea of what she was like from Lomax's description. She sounded athletic and vocal, in her twenties and very attractive. Attractive or not, Dale was ready to flirt with her.

Benfield came in sight, black and white houses leaning at odd angles against each other for support. Dale drove by the green and slowed near a bus stop to seek the entrance to the vicarage. An unadorned red-brick house stood back behind a shrubbery. He guessed that was it although ivy obscured the name on the gatepost. He turned his car into the entrance.

Dale tried the front doorbell twice. He could not hear it in the recesses of the house and walked to the back, thinking it probable the front door was seldom used. The back door was shut too and no one responded when his fist struck it.

The temptation to jump in the car and dash off home was strong. He was not eager to see Sheila, nor worried about lying to Lomax that he had soothed the vicar's wife. What forced him to stay was that he had told the police he was going to the vicarage and he did not want that ever to look like a lie. He must wait and see someone, ideally Mrs King but anyone would do to support his story if proof became necessary.

After circling the house Dale went through a gate at the rear into the churchyard. A missing vicar might well be in his church. He turned the ring latch and opened the door of St John's.

To begin with he believed the church empty and was backing out when he heard a scraping sound from some-where up high and looked up into the face of the Reverend Adam King. The vicar came down a ladder. He did not descend particularly to speak to Dale, whom he took for yet another visitor of which St John's had a good number, he appeared to have finished what he was doing. King said good evening and Dale said he had come to see Mrs King.

'My wife's not here, Mr Dale. She's had to hurry off to see someone rather urgently.' King recognized how the explanation tripped off the tongue. People so often turned to Jenny for help. 'Can I do anything for you?'

Dale thought not but he needed to establish his visit in

King's mind and the vicar seemed preoccupied. Dale could not think of anything else to say so he talked about *Angles*. He mentioned Jenny's visit to the office in Hertfield, said how seriously he regarded her complaint about the magazine getting into a young girl's hands and that he did not understand how it could have happened. He exaggerated his penitence to the point where he heard himself saying that the next issue would carry a warning to subscribers to avoid such a thing.

King was confused and Dale gathered this was the first he had heard of the matter. He asked the vicar to relay the apology to his wife but was told: 'You know, Mr Dale, it would be far better for you to speak to her yourself. She should be back soon.'

Dale agreed to wait a little while, saying it was an opportunity to look around the church and adding that he had read an item in a local paper about the carvings the vicar had discovered. Oddly, King did not want to discuss them and left Dale, saying he had a sermon to finish. Dale squandered ten minutes but Jenny King did not come and he drove off. He passed her yellow car, parked by a hedge, but he did not see Jenny.

Her husband bullied himself to concentrate on the last few points in the sermon and when it was done he flung down his pen and rose from his leather chair. The study was too cramped for pacing and he was restless with much to think about. He pulled open the door and went along the passage to the room Jeffrey Miles had used. A thrush was on the lawn. A cat skulked under the shrubbery. Rooks circled.

King drove a fist into his palm, his face contorted with frustration. In his mind he heard an echo of his voice, telling colleagues (showing off to colleagues?) at a meeting in St Albans: 'We've got the most amazing serpent. We're St John the Evangelist, you know, so the symbol is absolutely perfect.'

He had just found out they had not. They had an evil eye.

7

Dr Bourton did not welcome Jenny King's telephone call asking him to visit Mrs Pendle. He warned her he had an evening surgery to finish first and could not suggest how soon he might be free. To his mind it was obvious that if Mrs Pendle wanted his help she would have made the call herself. He did not begrudge home visits when a patient's condition demanded it but Jenny King was encouraging the woman to avoid the fact that she was not fit to live alone.

He was an elderly and querulous man but a competent doctor. He did not lose patients through negligence and they tolerated his manner because they knew they were in good hands. Some were scared of him but not Mrs Pendle so there was justification for his opinion that if she truly needed a house call she would have rung.

In this frame of mind he drove to Pendle Cottage on Friday evening. Three hundred yards up Back Lane, at the nearest cottage, weekenders were unloading their car and flinging open windows to air rooms. Dr Bourton noted smugly that the vicar's good lady could not be bothered to stay with Mrs Pendle until he got there. Her car was nowhere to be seen.

He simultaneously knocked and marched into the cottage. And was startled when Jenny King opened an interior door. 'She's in here, Doctor,' she said softly and thanked him for coming.

Mrs Pendle was in the back sitting room. The room had grown stuffy but she complained of feeling cold and would not have a window open. Jenny went into the kitchen while Dr Bourton examined his patient but the walls were thin and as she did not want to eavesdrop she let herself into the garden.

The air was refreshing although the hot, dry spell was unbroken and the grass yellowing. Jenny felt as if she had been in the small room for hours and had grown listless. Mrs Pendle needed more than company to keep up her spirits, she had deteriorated since morning.

Unusually, for she was not a morbid woman, she had brought up the subject of death. She wanted to die in her own home and repeated the theme until Jenny grasped that her friend was relying on her to remember this when the time came. Jenny had no qualms about reassuring her. She believed it to be every individual's right to do so. Mrs Pendle was a woman who'd had a say in the running of her life and was vexed that through incapacity she might be denied a say in the way she died. Jenny was prepared to make the point for her.

The matter came to a head much sooner than anticipated. Dr Bourton joined Jenny in the garden. 'I want to get her into hospital,' he said. 'She won't hear of it.'

Jenny was alarmed that things were so serious. She had expected a change of drug, perhaps a nurse dropping in. The doctor said: 'I want her to have tests. I can get her a bed for a few days, our hospital provision is among the best in the country. But she won't go.'

'I know she's distressed at the idea of going away from home,' Jenny ventured.

'*Distressed?*' said Dr Bourton as though the word were wholly inappropriate. 'She's a strong-minded woman, I know, but if you were to convince her she should co-operate it would be for her good.'

Jenny gulped and made a hash of saying what she had thought she had years to practise: that Mrs Pendle had the right to choose to go or stay; that she was not used to being pushed around; and that they shared a mutual trust and Jenny had promised her support.

'*Support?*' said Dr Bourton in the tone he had used for 'distressed'.

They wrangled. Jenny became entrenched and Dr Bourton angry in his failure to shift her. Indoors Mrs Pendle suffered her pain. She, naturally, had the final word when they both went back to her.

'Mrs Pendle, you're making a mistake,' said the doctor, impotent.

'No, Doctor, I'm making a decision,' she replied with a pained smile.

Shortly after that the doctor left. Jenny followed, on foot because her car had broken down on the way to Pendle Cottage. She had abandoned it by a hedge and it was too late to get the mechanic who lived in the village to start it. This was a nuisance but at least it had happened in Benfield and not miles out in the countryside. And she knew a short cut home, through the wood.

8

Jeffrey Miles had almost reached the wood when he discovered the yellow car. With each succeeding step his indignation grew. Jenny King was still looking for him!

He weighed his grey bag in his hand, wondering what to do. The bag was heavy because of the extra things he had bought and he'd had to hump it around all day. Until now he had intended to go straight to his camp and make it more comfortable. He had already done some work on it but there was scope for much more. Planning it had occupied him all the way back on the bus from Hertfield. The sight of the car plunged him into confusion.

Miles climbed the stile and stood still. Only the usual woodland noises reached him. His jaw tightened. That was what he had feared. She had not stopped to get leaves for flower arrangements or whatever it was her church women's groups did. She had gone to look for him.

He hid the bag in undergrowth and crept forward, his slight sounds masked by blackbirds rustling among friable fallen leaves. By now he knew the wood as well as anyone. Evening walks, while he was pretending to read at the vicarage, had made him familiar with it and two nights' camping had intensified the feeling that this was his territory.

Benfield wood was not a big one but it was nicely mixed woodland and few of the local people bothered to use it. If they ventured in it was to follow the path from the green to the church or to take one of its spurs to the rear of Church Cottages. Provided Miles kept away from paths he would probably never encounter anyone. If other tracks had ever existed – and the location of stiles suggested there might have been some – they had long disappeared through disuse. But Jenny had parked her car near one of those stiles. She was in his private part of the wood and his irrational resentment of her hardened. He froze, sensing movement ahead. Something was low down behind the broad trunk of a beech. Jenny was crouching, he guessed. She had seen him coming and hoped to catch him as he passed.

Miles edged nearer. The movement was not repeated. And then he was up to the beech but there was no one there. He cocked his head and concentrated, trying to gauge her direction. He heard what he hoped not to hear, foliage being disturbed to his right, where his camp lay.

His muscles contracted and breath became a pain in his chest. It was intolerable that she had forced herself on him at the vicarage and chased him around Hertfield and now she was breaking into his camp! With feline stealth he closed on her. She would not know he was near until it was too late.

His breath seemed to have stopped, it was so shallow. He glided, allowing no unnecessary movement. Everything in him was bent on confronting the woman. Trembling plants confirmed he was following where someone else had just passed but he had sited the camp so efficiently that he would be upon it before it was visible. And by then he would see Jenny, a flash of the pink outfit she had worn in Hertfield. Magenta would be the explicit signal that he had caught her.

His noiseless progress took time but he had to balance speed against secrecy and did not want Jenny scared away or given time to dream up a lie about her reasons for being in the wood. Miles felt he floated, so fluid were his movements.

He had marked a birch, a low-down, discreet mark to help him locate the camp if ever he were in doubt. He spotted the mark. Then he sped forward at a terrifying pace. Jenny had clearly gone inside the camp because he could see no magenta. He reached a new level of fury. *She had gone inside!* Everything was *spoiled*. He crashed into the camp, forcing over one of the flimsy branches which supported the tepee-like structure.

Confusion. A wild scream. One of the vicarage cats whisked by him and vanished among trees, scaring birds who sent their own panic skywards. There was no Jenny. No one.

When Miles was completely sure he went back for his bulging bag. In Hertfield he had bought a sleeping bag, a knife and a tin opener as well as food, knowing he could not risk the Benfield shop often because people would guess he was not living at Harpury. After a guarded check that Jenny's car was still by the hedge he returned to the camp. It was a mess. He had been congratulating himself all day that it was sound, snug and well camouflaged. But now he saw that he was wrong.

He set about gathering material to improve it, moving with considerable care and constantly aware of Jenny's possible proximity. But as time went on he cast around for other explanations for her leaving her car there and favoured in the end his invention that she had kept a secret meeting with the young man who had been friendly with her at the church, the man she called Don. Miles could not imagine any other reasons for her to tuck her car out of sight in a little-used lane and disappear.

The original structure of the camp had been flimsy. He had stuck three pieces of wood into the ground, leaning towards each other and capable of supporting the grass and bracken he had draped over them. It would not have lasted and he had been prepared to strengthen and extend it. Instead, he ripped out the two supports he had not sent flying in his rage and he started from scratch.

The site was the same, an excellent one because it was hidden by a low scrub oak and all around were bracken, shrubs and tangles uninviting to walk through and confusing to the eye. Miles hunted for a long piece of wood, a slender branch of about nine feet. He carried his prize back and lifted it into place by the oak, one end settled into the lowest fork and the other on the ground behind the tree.

It took much longer to gather the rest of the wood he needed, not because there was a shortage but because there was plenty and he was able to be selective. At the gardening counter of a shop in Hertfield he had bought a clasp knife and the garden twine he used to tie the shorter lengths of wood to the branch.

There was untying and adjusting to be done before he was

satisfied with the basic framework. The thing looked like a weird creature of the forests, its head up in the oak, its tail on the ground and legs splayed along each side. The 'legs' were four feet long near the head and diminished until the pair nearest the tail were stunted.

He cut ferns, leaving intact those nearest the tent to give fewest clues to his presence. He was hungry but light was dying and he had to press on. The torch he had bought would have to be used sparingly or he would give himself away. He spread ferns over the wooden frame, anchored them with twine and twigs and created a camouflaged tent. In the near dark he finished the job and crawled inside to strew more ferns as a floor and to savour his creation.

He sat there, arms hugging knees in a childish posture, insulated from night creatures and the curiosity of people. He was tired but very peaceful and secure. Nothing existed for him beyond the concealing thatch. He wanted to stay like that for always, deep in Benfield wood.

But there was more to do. He scrambled out of the tent and opened his bag to find food. There was brown bread and a wedge of meat pâté wrapped in cling film. Miles hacked at the loaf with his clasp knife and spread the pâté. Then he pulled the ring on a can of beer before opening a bag of tomatoes.

The tomatoes reminded him of Jenny and how, in the library, he had noticed a brown paper bag which had come from the greengrocer's where he had bought them. He could not read the lettering at that distance but the greengrocer's bags were printed with a winking cabbage and Miles saw a cabbage winking at him the length of the room.

Then he had seen a woman, bending by the bookshelves and heaving a heavy volume into place. In the time it took to register that only one person he knew wore magenta, she had got the book on the shelf and was straightening to see where to place others. Miles had been on his feet and moving.

Down the street. Never mind his washing in the launderette. Keep going. And he had. Not running because that attracted attention and, with every window plastered with posters of Mary Cross and asking honest citizens to report anything suspicious, he would not do that.

So he had ducked and dodged and met her again and sheered off down alleyways and lurked in men's toilets until futher delay was going to land him in other sorts of trouble. Finally he had sought sanctuary in the launderette and hidden his face in a magazine. Jenny was unlikely to go into a launderette because the vicarage had an efficient washing machine.

But it had been essential for him to complete his shopping. He had only had time to buy food and drop into the library, to see what the reference books could tell him about a basilisk, before he saw Jenny. Then he had lain low for hours, giving up any idea of working that day and hiding until he was sure Jenny would have left town. He spent the afternoon at the cinema and afterwards rushed around buying his sleeping bag and other essentials.

If the evenings had not been so light and long he would have caught an earlier bus but he worried about being seen heading for Benfield, traipsing down the lane towards the church at a time when he might reasonably be expected to be going the opposite way to Harpury. So he had lingered in Hertfield, in a café until the pubs opened and then in a pub because the cafés closed. The inconvenience had been worth it. He met no one and saw no traffic as he walked from the crossroads to the wood. And once he had rebuilt his camp he saw no reason ever to live anywhere else. Everything was perfect.

Some time later he groped for the torch and with its help collected the left-over pieces of wood and tidied the untidiness caused while building his tent. He carried most of the stuff away and buried it under bracken but he was loth to dispose of spare lengths of wood not needed for the supports. He had an idea they might be useful.

Apart from seeing Jenny he'd had another scare in Hertfield. There had been a lot of police. Miles had not liked that. No one approached him but he'd had the unpleasant feeling they might. He had never been questioned by the police, or no more rigorously than when Inspector Addison had gone to the vicarage after the murder, but he knew how doctors could probe and challenge. He imagined it would be the same as that.

9

A fox came near the tent early on Saturday morning. Its nearness woke Miles whose eyes opened to the rich colours and scent of the animal. The fox paused, paw lifted and ready to flee. It tilted its head, scrutinized a patch of bracken and sloped away. Miles lay still until long after. A quivering rabbit came into view, a squirrel darted from branch to branch and finches stirred in bushes. The wood was loud with birdsong.

Miles slithered out of his sleeping bag. The tent was tall enough to allow him to sit but that was all. He reached for a sweater. It was easier to put it on outside so he scrambled out, backwards. Then he walked away, looking for a place to designate as a lavatory.

After that he took stock. The tent had been comfortable. He had not woken once. From a few feet away it was still so well disguised it might escape notice. He realized this would change as the bracken died to brown but he planned to add new layers of covering to maintain the camouflage. Miles thought it a good idea to add an extra layer at once because when the weather changed he would need more warmth and the certainty that rain would not enter. The current structure, with ferns lashed upside down to ensure moisture ran off, would protect him from a shower but a heavy summer storm could force its way through.

He had chosen a green sleeping bag. There had been better ones but they were bulkier and they were not green. He dragged it out of the tent, turned it inside out to air and spread it on the ferns. Then he thought about breakfast: bread and honey, no butter because it might go rancid and anyway it would escape from its wrapping and be a nuisance. There were more cans of beer but nothing else to drink.

He regretted that but had only to survive Saturday and Sunday without. On Monday, when his presence in the village would be unexceptional, he could buy a soft drink at the shop. Jenny would supply him with tea and coffee while he worked.

Miles cleaned his teeth with beer and opened a can of cleansing pads bought at a chemist's. He wiped his face, neck and hands. On Monday he would have water because he still had access to the cloakroom at the vicarage as there were no facilities in the church itself. In addition there was a standpipe for cold water in the graveyard for people to fill flower containers or water plants if they chose. He had not seen anyone use it as few of the graves were decorated. If he could buy a Thermos flask in the village he would fill it at the standpipe. Otherwise he would use a beer can and buy a flask later when he made his next trip to Hertfield.

The church clock measured out Saturday as he cut bracken and gave the tent its extra layer, then flattened a beer can and dug into the soft ground among the ferns. He wanted a small pit where he could bury rubbish, such as the wrappings from his food, but the tool was inadequate below the first few inches. He went in search of a stone flat enough to gouge at the soil, remembering seeing something suitable. He found what he needed but instead of hurrying back to the pit he dared go to the edge of the trees. Jenny's car had gone.

On his way back it occurred to him that he would wear a path by repeatedly approaching the same way and that he could improve his security by creating a barrier. He worked out the detail while scraping the pit.

Saturday afternoon was the most hazardous time since he had come to Benfield wood. He heard children's voices and the bark of dogs wild in their freedom from small houses. Miles investigated, needing assurance that they were keeping predictably to the vicinity of the paths. It was true. He learned not to panic each time a fresh voice rang out.

Then there was a commotion from the direction of the church: voices and cars and much pealing of bells followed by more voices and more cars. It was a beautiful day for a wedding, so hot Miles was working without his shirt.

Towards the evening the sounds dwindled. There was a long peaceful stretch during which he finished the pit, buried accumulated rubbish and hid the flat stone conveniently close so he could use it to scoop earth on to layers of rubbish as the days went by. He cleaned his hands on grass, finishing off with another of the cleansing pads. They were scented and left his skin sticky. When he ate bread and pâté for his supper he swallowed lavender with each mouthful. Afterwards he opened a can of beer and read the paperback novel he'd had in his bag for weeks.

In the early evening there was another flurry of activity beyond the trees but no one came near him. He started on the barrier, moving a fallen branch to mask what might be an inviting path if a child or dog spotted it, stuffing bracken to block a possible way between shrubs, and coiling bramble to deter another approach. When light was poor he broke off and went for a stroll. At last the wood was his again, the intruders had gone away and he had it to himself.

He walked as far as the vicarage garden, electric light from the Kings' sitting room blinking through the shrubbery at him. Jenny still had not hung the curtains, presumably waiting for her husband to do it and afraid to mount the ladder herself. He did not go into the shrubbery, was not tempted. He had watched the couple from there before. It had been unavoidable as he had gone secretly to and from his room in the evenings, using his window as a doorway to the wood. The television would be on and the vicar would be sitting in a big old-fashioned chair with Jenny perching on the arm. His arm might be around her waist or hers around his shoulder. They would be touching. The Kings were always touching.

Miles had an idea. If the Kings were going to stay in their sitting room for long enough he could get to the churchyard unobserved and fill a beer can with water to drink. He could splash fresh water from the tap over his face and hands. He wanted very much to do that. He calculated the risk. If either of the Kings went to the church or out of the kitchen door they might glimpse him or hear the sound of water. If not, all would be well.

Avoiding the slight ditch, that was all that remained of a formal boundary between wood and garden, Miles pushed through the parted branches until he had a clear view. As the overhead light was on in the room there was no bluish glow of television but the Kings were sitting where he had pictured them, Jenny curled up in the chair and her husband lying on the carpet resting his head against it. She was stroking his hair. They were both looking in the same direction, to the corner where Miles knew the television stood. He ran back into the wood.

He fetched an empty can and was hurrying through the trees again when there was a short sharp sound quite close. Miles stopped dead, eyes glaring into the dusk. A softer sound followed. And then smoke. A cigarette.

Miles sidled behind a tree trunk and waited for more sounds, for the smoker to walk on. There was nothing. Then a slight stirring. Then only smoke. His fingers gripped the can so tightly it buckled. He *had* to get to the standpipe. He could not expect the Kings to sit for ever in front of the television and once they left that room he had no way of knowing where they were and whether he was safe. Before long the light would go and he could not make the journey in the dark. Equally, he dared not used his torch.

He wondered whether to retreat to the safety of his camp but hated being cheated out of the water now he had plotted a way to get it. Instead, he opted to skirt round the area where the smoker was and try to escape unheard and unseen. What bothered him was why the man was there. It was late. It was dark. It was away from the paths and the man was very quiet.

Miles thrust through the shrubbery for the second time. The Reverend Adam King was sitting in the chair. Jenny was nowhere to be seen. There was the sound of the back door opening and shutting and then she appeared in the lit room. Miles sighed relief: Jenny had been doing a small domestic chore like putting out milk bottles or taking rubbish to the dustbin. He saw her cross to the corner where the set stood and then move back, eyes on the screen, and sit down. He hoped the Kings were starting on a new programme and there would be no more popping in and out until he was safely away with his water.

He stepped back to start his journey past the house and through the gate from its rear yard to the churchyard. But at precisely that second a dark figure loomed about ten feet from him. Someone had crossed the corner of the vicarage garden while he was focusing on the Kings. It was a girl, making for the wood. Miles had no time for fear. He held his breath as she dashed by without noticing him although he could have put out a hand and touched her, if he had wanted to.

Miles knew who she was. Veronica Long. A stranger seeing him might have said nothing but if Veronica had she would have recognized him, wanted to talk and told everybody about it. He was shocked at how narrowly he had escaped discovery.

There were no more horrors on the way to the standpipe but when Miles reached it he found no water. Just as the disappointment seeped in, a light turned on upstairs in the vicarage alerted him to danger and he slunk away to the camp. Occasionally he stopped and sniffed but there was no warning smoke. He moved carefully forward, eyes straining and feet feeling for safe footing.

Guided as much by instinct as sight he reached the camp and sank down, exhausted and longing for a drink. He was ducking into the tent for a beer when he heard a woman's voice, close.

Miles was shaken beyond anything that had happened so far. Sweat broke on his skin, his heart raced. He was trapped. His camp had been found and he had walked into a trap. He crouched, eyes frantically searching the darkness.

The voice came again, a protesting murmur. Then another voice, a man's voice, a coaxing voice. The couple were no more than thirty feet from Miles, maybe less. He heard the woman's voice rise in renewed objection, just loud enough for him to know she was Veronica Long.

He cursed his naïvety at not suspecting the smoker was

hanging about to meet someone and that Veronica was dashing to him. Miles's fear was replaced by disgust, an emotion exacerbated by the intimate sounds that drifted across to him.

No wonder they had not heard him arrive, he thought as he dragged his bag out of the tent. They had been too engrossed with each other to suppose his movements signalled anything other than a wild creature or a cat from one of the cottages. He picked up his bag and melted away into the trees.

Veronica's home in Church Cottages could be reached from a spur of the main path through the wood and Miles deduced she would go back there soon. She could hardly spend the whole night in the wood with her lover. He supposed the man would walk her home and then strike out on his own. When they left the area of the camp they would be intent on finding a path, not wandering about in the wilderness. The chances of them blundering on the tent were negligible and if they did they would have no clue who lived there. Miles had his bag with him and that contained everything except the sleeping bag.

He circled, away from the tent but no further from the couple because he needed to hear when they left. A long time went by.

The church clock struck the hour and after that there were stirrings from where the pair lay. Miles peered across. The man was standing, his back to Miles. He was putting on a pale shirt, stuffing it into his trousers. Miles was wholly unprepared when the figure turned and faced him but then, as he bent to help the girl up, Miles scuttled away keeping low.

He was hampered by the bag, knew he was being noisy. Veronica gave a cry and the man made reassurances about foxes. Miles dived into a thicket and prayed for them to go. They walked straight to where he had waited for them and they kept going until their movement died in the distance. Veronica had not been taken to Church Cottages, she had been led off in the opposite direction. To Miles this was contradictory, even perverse. But the crucial thing was that they had gone and he knew to the edge of certainty that they had not discovered his camp.

He sat outside the tent, ears alert, until the clock struck the next hour. In all that time he heard nothing to raise his pulse. He pushed his bag into the tent, squeezed in after it and slept.

On Sunday morning Miles saw the fox again. More squirrels. More finches. He slithered out of the sleeping bag and made a thorough investigation before the villagers invaded his territory at their Sunday leisure.

A flattened area among the ferns showed him where Veronica and her lover had lain and he detected the path of his own ungainly flight from them. Vegetation was being broken or damaged at each coming and going. The wilderness was getting a used look. Miles could not see what to do about that although it worried him. Most people were reluctant to go where others had not already been, a primitive self-preserving instinct which applied to modern human beings who generally kept close to paths. The more feet that tramped through the wilder parts of Benfield wood, the more would come.

Miles blamed himself for not making the barrier to his lair more effective. He decided to circle it entirely, not merely stopping up the more inviting gaps, and with the clasp knife in his trouser pocket set out to cut more bramble.

This was dangerous because the bramble grew near cottages and he could be spotted. He was early enough to be lucky: back doors were closed, bedroom curtains still drawn.

The illusion of safety was shattered when a boy with a shotgun came through a garden gate. But the boy was looking up, thinking about rooks, and Miles flattened himself behind a tree while he went by. Then he snatched up his pile of bramble and walked rapidly away, deciding to take no more chances in that part of the wood in daylight.

Miles was curious to know why Veronica and her lover left the way they did, towards Back Lane. He followed their route, dawdling, taking a break from his work on the defences. Before he came to the perimeter of the wood he heard men and women talking, children arguing. Then he saw the cottages, a pair of semi-detached red-brick and flint cottages in an old Hertfordshire style. Each had a car parked outside it and youngsters and dogs running around. He could tell who they were: the weekenders.

He wondered which of the men had been with Veronica but could not work it out because none of them matched the male figure he had seen. Miles gave it up and walked parallel with the lane, unobserved.

A few yards on he came to the third cottage. This one had a name on the gate. Pendle Cottage. It stood alone, behind it fields and the distant roofs of Ayot St Martin. At first he thought it was empty. The gate was broken and there was no sound or sight of anyone. He wanted to check but decided it was the contrast with the weekenders' cottages, where windows and doors were wide open and people were spilling in and out, that gave the impression it was unoccupied. Water, he thought. That was behind his interest. He had been subconsciously thinking that if he entered Pendle Cottage he could get water.

Once he had realized this he started to walk on. A noise halted him. It came from the cottage. Something was rattling the letter box. He remembered Jenny mentioning that an old woman lived there and he assumed she kept a dog which was about to be let out. It would leap the steep bank from the lane and he would be found. Miles ran off, to the place where he felt safest.

During the afternoon he erected his defences, and lay in the sun, drank beer and read his book. That was an ideal time. He had made a small, perfect world. It would not be breached again by Veronica. For one thing, her lover would set off for London at any hour. No one else had strayed from the paths. Miles had only animals for company and that was all the company he required.

He took another stroll in the evening. The weekenders' cottages were shut up and their cars gone. He toyed with the idea of breaking in and getting water but it no longer seemed worth much effort. By morning he would be using the cloakroom at the vicarage. Pendle Cottage was silent, no anxious dog begging for a run.

Miles wandered casually, picking up heavy sticks which promised to be useful when he constructed an outer ring to his defences, something weightier and noiser than bramble to send him a signal if someone broke through. He was stooping for an excellent chunk of oak when a woman's flapping skirt attracted his attention. She had left the path and was bearing right, weaving between trees but keeping a certain course. If she did not veer she would be at the camp.

He could not bear it. After his hours of work disguising and protecting it, it was outrageous that anyone should march straight up to it. When she hesitated it was merely to lift her skirt over some of the things he had placed as a barricade.

Miles was devastated. With tears burning his eyes he moved after her. A few more yards and she would be close enough to the tent to see it for what it was. His pace quickened behind her. A shot rang out.

10

Roger Dale arrived at the *Angles* office on Sunday morning later than he had promised Al Lomax. He'd had a row with Sheila. He had not enjoyed walking away and leaving her hysterical but his time had run out.

Sheila had made him trundle around the shops with her on Saturday, too fearful of the killer allegedly hiding in Harpury woods to chance going on her own. She had said as much when her mother telephoned concerned for her safety.

Dale had been compliant, holding back the information that he would be out for a good part of Sunday. He had intended to tell her the lie on Friday evening but the rumour-mongers had come up with a new twist and Sheila accepted every menacing detail. She kept repeating how glad she was that Roger would be home all weekend and that perhaps the police would have caught the fiend by Monday so she would no longer be afraid to be left alone.

Dale said nothing while she chose a joint of lamb for Sunday lunch, nothing while she promised Caroline and Timothy that daddy would take them to Ashridge Forest on Sunday afternoon to make up for being near the house all week. On Sunday morning she found out.

He had positioned his briefcase in the hall because he expected to need a quick getaway when she became angry. She was in the kitchen, peeling potatoes, when he trotted out the lie that he had to go to Watford to interview a Brigges director who could not be reached the next week.

Sheila exploded. He attempted to leave the house while she screamed about him breaking his promise to the children and not caring that their lives were in danger. But when he started for the front door she got there first and grabbed the case. She forced her way past him and stumbled into the sitting room. Then she threw the case with all her strength. There was a tremendous crash as it smashed through the french window.

Dale raced through the kitchen into the garden, retrieved the case and fled through the side gate. The last he saw of Sheila she was howling on the sitting-room carpet. Caroline and Timothy were watching with the detached curiosity of children for whom the adult world is one of constant surprise.

Lomax was impatient, repeatedly looking at his watch. Dale dashed in.

'I thought you were never coming,' was all Lomax said. Dale mentioned being delayed at home and jingled his car keys to show he was raring to go.

Lomax said: 'We'll take my car.'

They did, with Lomax terse and Dale puzzled. He did not know much about what Lomax did when he was not at his engineering business or being dogsbody at *Angles*. They had met through a friend who knew Dale's project needed cash and Lomax had some to invest. The relationship had never developed into real friendship and had lasted longer than many partnerships of friends. Dale knew Lomax's wife had left him and taken the children the last time he was in trouble with the law but what the trouble was, how Lomax lived now, were mysteries.

Neither did Dale question his present mood in case Lomax had learned that he had not seen Mrs King and mollified her. After the fight he would be ready to argue about *Angles* but until then would risk nothing that might jeopardize his introduction to the fight scene.

Lomax cut through bluebelled lanes, finally slowing at a pub standing alone beside a common. He had spoken scarcely a word and when he tugged on the handbrake all he said was: 'There's a back room.'

Dale went into the porch. There was only one door from that but on the other side of the bar was another which was closed. He bought drinks, a pint of beer for himself and a brandy for Lomax. Then they waited, Lomax inspecting the crowded room for familiar faces and Dale checking that no one was taking a special interest in either of them. Satisfied, Lomax tipped his head in the direction of the closed door.

A knot of men lounged in front of it. Lomax asked them to make way and when they did not budge added, 'Come on, mate. We're looking for Alfie.' He spoke very low, nobody outside the group could have heard. The men made just enough gap for Lomax and Dale to squeeze through.

In the back room were about twenty men, two of them playing pool. Eyes flicked towards Dale and Lomax but no one stopped talking or turned and the cues continued to click against the balls.

Dale expected to meet someone called Alfie but never did because Alfie was the password. He liked that touch and the secret clubby atmosphere in the room. He was not one of them yet but was on the verge of initiation, a time to be savoured for its own special excitement. He felt again like a boy learning about sex: he knew it went on, he knew people who did it and at last it was his turn. Subsequent thrills could be repeated but not the act of discovery.

Men were introduced only by first names or nicknames. Dogs were not mentioned directly, making the talk tricky to follow. Some of the men appeared to be owners and Lomax took his drink over to talk to one, Rex, a sharp-faced gypsy type.

The men were a complete social mix: Rex at the scruffiest end of the scale and Joe, who had the manner of a prosperous alderman, at the other. There were East End accents and public-school ones, Campari drinkers and brown-ale men, old and young. And over it all was the smell of the excitement of the illicit. Dale felt privileged to be there, a newcomer in a secret society with its rituals of protection. Practised in deceit, he saw himself as a natural member.

He was too wise to blunder in with questions. He asked nothing and gratefully received what was given. As Al's friend he was accepted. Things had begun well and pleasurable ripples of anticipation were running through him.

But suddenly there was a scare, a warning kick on the door and alarm filled the room. A catch on a window snapped across, the casement swung and two men escaped into the orchard. Others grabbed cues and crowded to the table, ostensibly concentrating on the play. The players potted and clicked. Men snatched up darts and one began to throw. Dale noticed for the first time the phoney score chalked on the board in readiness.

The cover was unnecessary. A rhythm of taps on the door indicated that danger was over. Everyone relaxed a shade. One of the loungers came in from the bar and whispered that a couple of plain-clothes detectives had been in the bar. They had taken their drinks to the bench in front of the pub so they were going to be around a while.

Rex and Joe were among those who decided they should play for safety. 'It's that Hertfield murder,' said Joe grinding out a cigar. 'This area won't be safe until the police have solved it and gone home.'

Dale was cruelly disappointed. The fight was cancelled. They could all drink up and, in unobtrusive numbers, leave the pub. Lomax, seeing his face, said: 'Don't blame us, Roger. Blame the chap who killed Mary Cross.'

'That photo on the poster,' began a man standing near. 'It's a photo of her dead body. It said so in the papers. They do that if they don't know who a person is and can't get a proper picture. The morticians must . . .' People quickened with interest, but not Lomax. He swallowed the last of a whisky which Dale took as a signal that he was ready to go. But the dark man cornered Lomax for a rapid discussion which ended with Lomax nodding agreement. He was to go to Rex's house straight away and that meant Roger Dale had to go too.

During the journey Lomax was less taciturn than earlier. Rex, he explained, was the man offering him a share in a dog. Several of the men had described it as a promising young animal. Rex wanted him to take a look at it and make up his mind. Lomax told Dale to cheer up: he would not get a fight that day but at least he would see a dog.

He drew into a lay-by and left the engine idling. 'Rex will

be along in a minute,' he said. 'He came another way to avoid us being seen together.'

Dale appreciated the wisdom of such precaution. No one was confident that the police at the pub were off duty and unaware of the gathering in the back room. He had already grasped some of the rules of this secret society: they never met at the same pub twice; they made arrangements late and made them discreetly; only when they were together and sure there were no interlopers did they say where that day's fight would be held; and as they moved around they were equally circumspect.

Rex flashed his van lights once and drove by. Lomax started after him, keeping well back but getting occasional sightings of the cream van on the twisting road. Eventually Rex slowed for a turn. Then he went into the entrance of a small-holding. The house was tarred clapboard with white window frames and geraniums in a tub by the front door. Everything was prettily rural and innocuous.

But they did not go into the house. In a black barn behind it Rex showed them Havoc. Dale acknowledged the aptness of the dog's name but his words were obliterated by the noisy ferocity of the caged animal.

The barn stank with the dog's odour. His body thudded against steel bars. But gradually he subsided, grumbling away to a corner. In the comparative calm Dale heard the cries of swallows cutting through air to nests among the beams.

Rex was looking at his dog with proprietorial pride. Lomax was stifling an unbusinesslike admiration. Dale spoke: 'So that's an American pit.'

Havoc had been bred for fighting and Rex's claim that his sire was one of the reigning champions encouraged him to ask several thousand pounds for a half share. 'They're getting rarer and the price will go up, not down,' he said in a flat London accent. And elaborated for Dale, the newcomer: 'The Customs and Excise know the difference between these and Staffordshire or English bull terriers these days and stop them coming in. It's not like it was a few years back when they were all pretty little puppies and no one was any the wiser.'

He did not refer to the court cases which had brought the

revival of the medieval sport to public attention and made customs officers increasingly vigilant. Instead he showed off the strength of the pup's jaws. He dangled a piece of wood attached to a leather strap and when the animal clamped on it Rex swung Havoc around.

'His sire,' said Rex wiping sweat from his face afterwards, 'bit his way though concrete to escape from a cage. I tell you, Al, this little fellow's tough.'

Lomax grunted. He sauntered round to the other side of the cage. Rex followed, still pouring out his sales talk.

Dale caught Havoc's eye and the dog trotted to the front of the cage. His jaws were disproportionately large, his coat light and his ears cropped. Full grown he would be a monster of around sixty pounds. But there was no possibility, even at this stage, of confusing him with any other breed, such as Mrs Catesby's fuddled old Staffordshire, Rusty.

Havoc grew sour. He hurled himself at the bars, growling, and sent Dale back a pace or two. Dale thought he radiated power and courage and that Lomax would be a fool to turn down such a chance. His frustration at seeing the dog cooped up instead of in action was acute and Rex's demonstration had been inadequate to show the nature of the beast.

Lomax and Rex came back, Rex saying: 'You'd recoup the outlay easily, Al. He'll be a winner every time.'

Lomax had still not said yes. Rex decided to show him more. The dog went willingly on to the treadmill, a six-foot-diameter contraption at the end of the cage. Then Rex left the barn. Havoc's quivering anticipation turned to frenzy when Rex brought a freshly killed pup and hung it up just out of reach.

'Builds his strength,' Rex shouted to Lomax. 'And you can see he already knows what dogs' flesh is for!'

Beneath the dead pup a dark patch was spreading in the dawdust. Hot blood mingled with the stink of Havoc and, coupled with the violent noise, made Dale sick and heady. Revulsion gave way to thrill, to a stirring of deep-buried responses which were essentially sexual. Dale prayed Lomax would say yes.

Rex stooped for a handful of sawdust and rolled it in his

76

hands to cleanse them of blood. He brushed the last of the sawdust off against his trouser legs and, as words were useless against the volume of the frantic dog, gestured to Lomax and Dale to follow him out.

The house was empty and skimpily furnished but there was a video recorder and Rex drew up some tatty chairs. He wanted to show Lomax Havoc's sire in the pit. What he had was a poor-quality copy of an amateur video, all camera shake and badly focused. There was no sound but there was colour and a great amount of blood. The champion tore the challenger apart but when the contest seemed to be ending too swiftly a man with a stick like a sharpened cricket stump forced its jaws open and allowed its victim respite before the pit was free to continue the slaughter. In Rex's room there was no sound except for the hastened breathing of the three men.

Dale went outside when it finished, saying he would like some air and leaving Lomax and Rex to finalize a deal. He sounded calm but the video had brought on a familiar restlessness. His mind lingered on the bloodiest moments and he cursed the police whose arrival at the pub had ruined his chance of seeing the real thing.

'Well?' he asked Lomax as they drove away from the small-holding.

Lomax's puffy face was smiling but all he said was: 'One or two details to sort out yet.'

They parted in Hertfield and Dale got into his car. Once Lomax was out of sight he got out again and let himself into the *Angles* office. He had an idea for a sequence with a girl and a dog, using dog fighting as a theme. Of course, he would be unable to use an American pit. That would be far too dangerous even if he knew one. Anyway, it was the theme that counted, not documentary accuracy. Any terrier of a tough breed would do as long at it was obedient. He wished Mrs Catesby's Rusty would come home.

Dale browsed through some girlie magazines he kept in the office to provide inspiration for *Angles*. He found several ideas he could adapt. The problem would be getting the right degree of menace. Get it wrong and it would either look like shots of a girl visiting Crufts or else like the basest depravity.

There was a local woman he might use again. She had to be paid but it was not much and she would save him the trouble of picking up a girl and wheedling her to do what he wanted. Wendy could be relied on. He cast about for her telephone number, planning to win her agreement and find a dog later. If she refused he would think about a different sequence altogether.

The Sandra Sutton pictures might be good enough as a stand-by, he thought. But when he went into the darkroom for the prints left drying on Friday, he discovered they had been ripped up.

Lomax. Nobody else could have got near them. So *that* was it. That was why Lomax had been offhand. He had taken a dislike to the Sandra Sutton pictures and chosen to say so in this way.

Dale scooped the pieces from the floor into the palm of his hand and carried them to the desk. Sandra Sutton had become a jigsaw. He found a corner piece. Then he matched its jagged edge with the fragment showing the girl's unfortunately childlike nose. Slowly he put her together again, until the four prints were as whole as they could ever be and she smiled provocatively through the wreckage. He toyed with the idea of using the jigsaw theme in one issue, tearing a print and scattering pieces through the pages for readers to snip out and assemble the picture.

Then he telephoned Wendy, but the man she lived with was home and she could not talk openly. She offered to meet Dale that evening. He spent the intervening time making more prints of Sandra Sutton and writing items for the next *Angles*. Then he walked to the Red Cow.

On the way he imagined Wendy sitting cross-legged on a bar stool so that the shapeliness of her calves caught the eye of every man who entered. Wendy used to be a barmaid, the type whose working clothes had low necklines and body-hugging skirts regardless of fashion's mood. Out of fashion, she was less glamorous than tarty.

But Wendy was late and Dale waited most of an hour before she teetered through the door in her patent high heels. Pete, she apologized, had not gone out as early as she expected. Until he went she had been unable to slip away. 'I've left the kids,' she said, comparing her marcasite watch with the pub clock. 'Anyway, why shouldn't I? They're his kids, not mine. Thanks.' She took the gin and tonic the barman pushed across to her before he went to another room and left them alone.

Wendy hopped on to the bar stool and crossed her legs. 'Well, then, Roger,' she said. 'What's this about?' She knew full well it would be work, he would not have dragged her out of the flat to waste her time.

He told her. The light of interest died in her eyes. She murmured doubtfully. Her previous sessions with him had been simple stuff, just her without her clothes and him with his camera. She could not pinpoint the precise difference but her intuition warned her off.

Dale assumed she was thinking about the money. He said: 'It might take a bit longer than the other times. I'd pay you more, of course.'

'You'd have to pay me more, anyway. I put the rates up.' She gave a challenging smile.

He understood they were to go on pretending Wendy had a modelling career, that his occasional sessions did not represent the bulk of her work. She liked to claim she was astute but it was demonstrably untrue. How had she let Pete lure her into his flat and make her responsible for his children when everyone in Hertfield knew he had another mistress a couple of streets away? Dale asked what was bothering her.

Wendy said: 'I've heard you should never act with animals.'

For a split second he thought she was joking. He recovered in time to treat the point seriously, reassuring her that she would not be upstaged by the dog. It was another of Wendy's conceits to regard the business of modelling as a branch of the acting profession although she had been no nearer to that than she had to a glossy gatefold. Once, after photographs, wine and sex, she had reminisced about an encouraging notice in a local paper for her part in a charity review.

Talking Wendy into posing for the dog sequence took time, far more time than a woman who had left three children untended should have spared. Eventually guilt surfaced. 'Ring me when you've fixed the rest,' she said and left.

Dale had another drink before following her out. The warm evening air reminded him how hungry he was but the Red Cow did not provide food on Sundays. With a pang he remembered Sheila and the state she had been in when he drove out of Harpury. It was the first thought he had given her for hours and it was prompted purely by the realization that he could not rely on a meal being put in front of him when he got home.

Down a side street near the Red Cow was a pub with a microwave oven and the promise of hot pies at any time. Dale ate one before heading for his car.

He drove carefully, having drunk far too much to be safe, but it did not occur to him until he was leaving Hertfield behind that it would be more prudent to spend the night in the office. He had done it once before, turning back after beginning the journey, but could not bring himself to do so now.

Hedges blurred at the fringe of his uncertain vision yet the car felt sluggish. Dale pressed the accelerator, releasing it marginally too late as he neared a long bend. Surprisingly, the car was suddenly on the wrong side of the road. He brought it back to the left as he came out of the bend, took his foot off the pedal and let the speed drop while he worked out what was wrong with the steering.

After several hundred yards he put the blame on the camber of the bend although this was not something that had ever troubled him before. In case the problem recurred further along the road he went deliberately slowly.

A couple of cars overtook him. A few passed in the opposite direction. Otherwise the road was quiet and he expected to roll gently home without interruption. But before long he could sense another effect of the beer. He had to stop and relieve his impatient bladder.

A wood lay ahead on his left and he planned to pull into the side of the road as soon as he reached it. He overshot the exact place he had in mind but it did not matter. Dale got out.

Returning from the trees he discovered he had left the car

engine running. When he tried to move off it stalled. What happened next shook him into a semblance of sobriety. Up the road behind him streaked a white car with a flashing lamp. Dale drove on, his eyes on the pursuer in the rear-view mirror. 'Keep calm,' the voice in his head instructed. 'Keep moving steadily on.'

He was already imagining the way the car would swoop by, how he would see its brake lights come on before it was stationary and a policeman was in the road waving at him to stop. He had been through it. He knew exactly what would happen – unless the police forgot about breathalyser bags and accused him of killing Mary Cross.

Dale's hands tightened involuntarily on the steering wheel. His right foot ached to be allowed to jab the accelerator that could take him away out of danger. But the voice inside argued that it would be folly, that he had better do nothing. Grit his teeth and do nothing.

His rear mirror was full of the flashing car. Then its white shape was alongside him and Dale was refusing to acknowledge it with so much as a glance. Sweat ran down his body. He was trembling.

To his amazement the car did not overtake. It spun away to its right. Just as he grasped that it had turned down a lane he heard a clamour. Fire engines. Roaring out of Hertfield, after the fire officer whose car was confusingly like a police car, came two fire engines. He was not about to be arrested after all.

11

A shot rang through Benfield wood. Jeffrey Miles recoiled, the reverberating sound terrifying him. He grazed his arm against a tree as he staggered back but did not notice.

Then he found himself on all fours, bolting through undergrowth until he came to impenetrable vegetation and squatted there, gunfire ringing in his ears and his heart pumping panic.

He struggled to clear his head, to listen for the approach of his enemy. High above birds were whirling and screaming, their confusion as great as his own. Miles reached out to the greenery close to him but there were no useful sticks, no weapons. He had gone headlong into a trap. There was only one way out and he was defenceless.

But he knew Benfield wood. He had a chance. Calmer now, he could choose his direction. He would play hide and seek and the odds would be in his favour – if only he could break from the trap.

Miles held his breath, turning his head carefully from side to side so that his eyes and ears would miss no sign. When he was sure, he crawled forward a few yards, rose to a crouching position like a sprinter waiting for the starting pistol, and then ran. He hurdled fallen branches, plunged through bracken, forced his way round huddles of bushes and got deep among the trees.

At last he felt safe enough, brave enough. Protected by a tree trunk he rose to full height and peered around. A squirrel descended an adjacent beech and took off in alarm as Miles tensed. Wood pigeons resumed their murmuring and a rabbit popped out of a burrow.

Eventually he dared to inch his way towards the camp. The initial shock was receding but he was confronting another horror: his perfect world was ruined, all his efforts wasted. Intense anger forced tears that burned and blinded. He rubbed a fist into his eyes, streaking his grubby face. Through the blur he saw something on the ground, beyond the bramble defence which had proved no defence. He picked up a canvas shoulder bag.

It was unzipped and things tumbled from it as he lifted it. A comb. A purse. Cigarettes and matches. A diary. The woman he had chased had dropped her bag. Miles stuffed things back, pocketing only what was useful to him, and tossed it into the pit. With the flat stone he filled the pit with soil, hurled the stone far into the braken, disguised the pit with ferns, and went to the tent. He was sobbing as he dragged out his holdall and squashed his sleeping bag into it.

Then he attacked the tent. First he kicked and smashed at the tallest supports until they cracked or grew loose. He crushed and wrecked until the perfect shape he had striven for was destroyed. The tent remained standing, the long branch firm against the fork of the scrub oak and a cavity beneath the bracken covering. Miles ripped the diary and put the pieces into the cavity. He fetched handfuls of brittle leaves and twigs and threw them in too.

After that he carried his bag a hundred yards away and hid it before setting light to the torn pages. He expected to have time to do the rest and went around the defensive ring trying to ignite the materials piled there for protection. One or two caught but the rest were stubborn. Only his tent smoked, smouldered and flared.

For a minute or two he watched the pyre of his happiness. A savage rage pounded his skull. Abruptly he turned his back and walked north. The camp had been no good. It had not protected him. It had been irrevocably sullied by intruders and he had been powerless.

St John's clock was striking as the jagged line of gravestones came into view. A blackbird was singing from the tiled roof of the church porch. Miles turned the ring latch of the ancient door.

Sunday. Late on Sunday evening and the only evidence that the church had been peopled earlier was a change of hymn numbers on the board and fresh flowers in vases. Miles left his bag in a pew and climbed the ladder to his platform. The panels were shadowed. Miles ran his fingers over the form of the basilisk.

He wanted to draw from it comfort, to be warmed by the magnificent creature and its distant creator. But this time there was no eruption of his emotions, no conviction that another spirit had entered him. The stone was harsh and cold to his hands.

It had never disappointed him before. He accepted the failing as his own, blaming the turmoil of his mind for an inability to respond. Even so, he stayed with the carving for a long time, hoping. When he roused himself he had trouble finding the ladder and the church below was a black void which gave him the sensation that everything but he and the basilisk had been destroyed.

Miles got his torch from his bag. The beam could be used as a pinpoint and he could not risk more. Using the thin blade of light he explored the church, pretending he had never seen it before and steering his thoughts away from things he would rather not dwell on.

The Dornaye monuments were far less impressive viewed in this way, the Arthur Bellerman memorial unexciting. Everything was dulled and flattened. Miles forced himself on, bullied himself to shut the terrible events out of his mind.

He read the plaque naming Benfield's fallen men of two world wars. He studied the banner in the chapel and he drew his light along embroidered kneelers in a pew. Then he browsed through the leaflet about St John's, thinking someone would have to rewrite it once his carvings were acclaimed. Beside the pile of leaflets and the donation box was the visitors' book. Miles opened it at January and picked out names and the places from which people had travelled.

January had been a cruel month and there were hardly any entries. February was an improvement although the visitors were predominantly Hertfordshire people. March and April were quiet times too although during the week of the schools'

Easter holiday numbers mounted and addresses were farther afield.

By May, when the woods were rich with bluebells, there were many more. At weekends the pages were crowded but a handful of visitors had straggled in on other days of the week. Miles trailed his light across their names, wondering how many of them would trouble to come back when his carvings had brought Benfield fame.

The light stopped moving. Then it flickered around an entry as Miles's hand trembled. He steadied himself, took a pen from his pocket and scored through a name. Then he shut the book and snapped off the light.

The memory of light made red circles in the blackness before him. He switched the torch on again, pointed it low and carried his bag to the tower. Dropping the bag in the bell loft he went up the rest of the stairs. He had not been to the top before but guessed the access to the roof would be easily opened because the Kings, either through laxity or policy, left everything accessible. Miles was right. The trap swung at his touch and he looked up at the sky.

The night was warmly overcast and the moon young. He was glad. No one would see him. He wondered whether to unroll his sleeping bag under the stars but delayed a decision. Leaning his forearms on the stone parapet he discovered a tender area. In the darkness he felt the damage, fingertips describing to him the torn skin and congealed blood. He thought about trying to clean it with one of his pads but they were impregnated with a spirit he knew would sting. He made no decision about that, either.

Miles remained on the tower, his fury at the desecration of his camp subsided and his mind occupied with minor, present, issues. And he was standing there, looking down at the vicarage where light shone through bedroom curtains, when Benfield wood exploded into flame.

His hands gripped the rim of the tower and he smiled an exultant smile that stayed with him all the time the fire surged unnoticed; and while people ran from cottages; and while fire engines hurtled from Hertfield; and while every vestige of his camp and a great deal of the wood went up in smoke.

The sky was lit. Miles picked out individual trees; rabbits and a fox running for their lives through the churchyard; the Reverend Adam King dashing out of his back door in a dressing gown; and Jenny haring down the street to Church Cottages. If anyone had chanced to look up at St John's they would have seen Jeffrey Miles, a monstrous gargoyle, laughing at the destruction and willing it to go on and on and on.

12

They slept late at the vicarage on the morning after Benfield wood burned. Jeffrey Miles met no one but a cat as he went to the cloakroom. What he saw in the mirror above the washbasin astonished him. He had dressed in a clean shirt and fresh trousers but immediately tore them off and took a shower.

Jenny had put out only a hand towel since he stopped living there and he had to manage with that. He had no shampoo with him and rubbed toilet soap over his hair as well as his body. In the camp he had used his battery-operated electric shaver but staying clean shaven had given him a misleading impression of his appearance.

Miles draped the soaking towel on its rail and opened the window wide to encourage the room to dry fast. Then he went back to the church still without seeing the Kings. He felt much better for the shower although he had accidentally rubbed his tender arm and then had trouble washing the blood out of the towel.

While he opened up a new panel, he returned to the problem of where to live. He was tempted to try another camp in a different wood, believing his mistake had been to build close to a village. If he took a bus up the Harpury road he might find a wood away from habitation and settle there undisturbed. Then he could come and go by bus each day and not arouse suspicion if he were seen.

But camping without a means of keeping clean was not going to work. He had been enormously lucky to get to the cloakroom unseen that morning and could not hope for that degree of luck to be repeated. Miles tried to think of a way round the problem because the dream of a woodland tent was very attractive. Finally he hit on the idea of buying himself swimming trunks and using the pool at Hertfield. That was the town's pride: a large modern pool with hot showers for use before and after swimming. Miles was an indifferent swimmer but prepared to pay the entrance fee if it would secure him a shower. He made up his mind to spend Monday night in the church tower and then look for a more private wood to build a better camp.

In the vicarage the Kings were arguing. A group of people from the Arthur Bellerman Society in Virginia, USA, were due to visit the church the next day and the vicar had discovered that his wife did not mean to meet them or offer tea.

'I'm not a tourist attraction, Adam!' Jenny scrubbed at his breakfast plate where egg had congealed.

He said petulantly. 'You've known for weeks that they were coming.'

'Have they actually asked you to feed and water them?'

'No, but they're making a trip out here from London. They'll expect something.'

'Fine.' She set the plate down noisily. 'You give them something. Tea. Scones. Whatever you feel like laying on.'

He saw they were getting nowhere. He had never expected Jenny to settle for sewing circles and flower-arranging clubs but he had assumed she would be cook, hostess and washer-up whenever he had guests. Usually she was, but the Arthur Bellerman Society had shifted the day of its visit and now it clashed with her keep-fit club.

'Look, Jenny,' he said patiently. 'Can't you get someone else to run the class? Just for one afternoon?'

'It's not easy for women with small children to make a commitment for a whole afternoon a week but they're doing it. How can I let them down?'

He took a deep breath. 'The reason you can do it is that you've never done it before. They'll understand it's a crisis.' The words were spoken before he realized how lame they would sound.

Jenny did not let him escape. 'What sort of a fool does that make you look, if you're not capable of asking them to help themselves to a few scones and mince pies?'

Ah, he thought. It was going to be all right. They were going to get mince pies too. Jenny was good at mince pies.

She threw a teatowel on to its hook. 'I'll do some mince pies this evening. I'll ask Mrs Long to make some scones – hers are better than mine. And I'll see whether she'd like to serve and wash up. You'll get me for ten minutes, Adam. I'll dash up from the village hall and make the right noises to the Arthurs and then I'll run right back again. Will that do?'

He said it would. He poured them both mugs of coffee while Jenny rounded up washing to go in the machine. He had an empty day ahead. He decided to inspect the damage to the wood and call on one or two people whose cottages near the green had been threatened during the fire. Later he would read through the information he had on Arthur Bellerman so he did not make gaffes when he met the Virginians.

Jenny came back, a bundle of clothes pinned under one arm and towel in her hand. 'I think Jeff took a shower this morning. The cloakroom's wet and this towel is wringing.' She showed him. She still sounded cross.

'It doesn't matter, does it?' Winning the argument had put him in a more relaxed frame of mind.

'Well, it's a bit odd, Adam. He chooses not to live here any longer but he wants to shower.'

He pushed a mug across the table towards her. As she raised it to drink she asked whether he had poured one for her to carry over to Miles. He had not so she did it herself. Before taking it out she filled the washing machine and switched it on. Her husband thought she had overlooked the cloakroom towel but she took a bowl and put it to soak in biological powder. She was playing safe. It was a new towel and she suspected the mark on it was blood.

'He probably cut himself shaving,' suggested King.

Jenny opened her mouth to say he could not have done. Jeff used an electric shaver. She had heard it often enough. But her husband was saying: 'Don't refer to any of this when you take the coffee over. You know how twitchy he gets if he thinks we're being nosy.'

'Especially me, you mean.'

He gave a sympathetic smile because Miles's interpretation of Jenny's behaviour was plain ridiculous. He said: 'Jenny, if he'd asked you whether he could have a shower, what would you have said?'

She pulled a face. Of course she would have said yes. 'All right,' she told Adam. And wondered whether to leave a bath towel in the cloakroom in future or whether Miles might resent that too.

After delivering the coffee and telling Miles about the drama of the fire Jenny had to rush away. Oversleeping after the broken night was going to make her late all day and she had a lot to cram in. First, Mrs Long.

The woman was not at home and Jenny went to the village shop in pursuit of her. She bought things for herself, including flour for the mince pies and scones, and waited until Mrs Long had completed her shopping and her chat with the shop-keeper. They walked back together, at a snail's pace compared with Jenny's usual speed. Mrs Long agreed to bake the scones and generally help on Tuesday afternoon. 'Do you want Veronica too, Jenny? I'm sure she'd come. She's not doing anything else.'

Veronica never was, apart from the day she received her dole money and took the bus into Hertfield and met a friend. For a spell Veronica had worked in a factory but it had not been a real job, only what politicians called work experience. After it Veronica got no more work. She did not seem to care as it had not been a happy experience.

Before they reached Church Cottages Jenny assured Mrs Long there would be no more copies of *Angles* coming through her door. The editor had promised. Mrs Long marvelled at what wonders the vicar's wife was able to perform, what authority she had.

Home again, Jenny set off for Back Lane. The mechanic who lived on the green had patched up the car but warned her to take it to a garage for a service soon. She roared off as though he had sworn it would run for ever.

Niggling at the back of her mind all morning was her failure to go to Mrs Pendle during the fire. The wind had not been blowing towards Pendle Cottage but the woman might have been alarmed. Jenny had been terribly busy helping create a fire break before the fire brigade arrived and then comforting the more tremulous villagers who stumbled dazed on to the green or appeared as anxious faces at bedroom windows.

She had decided that Dr Bourton's new pills would allow her friend to sleep through the excitement and had neither called nor telephoned. Curving along Back Lane she confirmed that the blackened part of the wood was out of sight and it was very likely Mrs Pendle still knew nothing of the fire.

She opened the broken gate, recalling her forgotten promise to fetch a hammer and nails to fix it. Next time, she vowed. Definitely next time. She rattled the letter box and called out, then turned the handle. The door did not yield.

Mrs Pendle locked up at night and unlocked in the morning. Jenny guessed she had either slept very late or was ill. Checking was easy enough, she had a front door key.

It was unmarked, among the clutter on the shelf in the car. She fished through the oddments and found keys to three local doors. The large old-fashioned one belonged to the cottage. Jenny unlocked the door and found Mrs Pendle dead.

The body was in the passage, right behind the door. It was cold. She stepped over it and grabbed the telephone. The receiver had swung down to the floor from a table. She jiggled the rocker, got a dialling tone, got Dr Bourton.

Jenny did not like to touch Mrs Pendle. She believed one was not supposed to although she could think of no reason for that. After all, Mrs Pendle could not be harmed.

Waiting for the hum of the doctor's car along the lane, she prepared herself to meet his accusing eyes. She remembered with shame her own inadequate argument against his urging that Mrs Pendle went to hospital. And remembered with more comfort the exchange between doctor and patient: *'You are making a mistake.' 'No, I am making a decision.'* They could, naturally, be the same thing.

Dr Bourton drove from Ayot St Martin in what seemed hours but was inside thirty minutes. Jenny imagined his patients at the surgery sighing and shuffling with irritation as they waited for him to come back. He turned Mrs Pendle's body over with as much care as if she had been alive and in pain. Then he made some telephone calls and finally turned to Jenny. 'When did you last see her?'

Jenny felt her colour rise. 'Saturday afternoon.'

He nodded as though she had confirmed a dreadful suspicion. He did not look at her again. She wanted to scream at him that she was no more responsible for life and death than he was and that getting Mrs Pendle to hospital might not have altered to a fraction of a second her allotted span. She clenched her teeth to control herself before asking: 'What happened?'

Dr Bourton made a gesture at the corpse, on its back now and with a livid face turned to the ceiling. 'Coronary thrombosis,' he said and opened the front door.

Jenny crossed over the body and kept up with him. She was at his elbow as he went down the path saying he had arranged for collection of the body.

'What should I do?' she asked as he got into his car.

He started the engine. He said: 'I have no idea, Mrs King. Mrs Pendle confided her wishes to you, not to me.' She had to move back sharply as he pulled away.

In the cottage again she averted her eyes from the body, uncertain whether she ought to cover the face or whether that was a muddled idea. She stooped to pick up a key, checking that her own was in the lock and this must have been Mrs Pendle's. Jenny put it on the table by the telephone and rang the vicarage. Adam would know what to say, what she ought to do. He was remarkably good like that. A talent for comfort, his mother called it. The vicarge telephone rang and rang but Adam was not there.

Pulling herself together she prepared to wait until the people, whoever they were, came to take the body wherever bodies were taken. She brushed aside Dr Bourton's hurtful manner and thought there was some truth in his words. Mrs Pendle *had* talked to her long ago about such intimate details as how her body and her property were to be disposed of. And had she not pointed out a chest where she kept a metal box containing papers?

Jenny went upstairs. In a bedroom at the front of the house was a Victorian mahogany chest, in a top drawer the tin containing an insurance policy, bank books, a building society account book and other documents including details of Mrs Pendle's solicitor in Hertfield.

She telephoned the solicitor who asked her to see him that afternoon. Then she made other phone calls cancelling what until then had been her plans for the day. One of those was secret and she shelved that too: she had intended to go to Harpury and follow up R. Dale to see whether he was the R. Dales of *Angles*. Adam's account of a visit from the editor had made her more interested, not less. The man had been overreacting and she was intrigued to know why. She did not for a moment believe he would publish a warning to his readers to hide the publication. Editors did not do that kind of thing.

Cecil Payne Mallory was a senior partner in the solicitors' practice. He had known Mrs Pendle for much of her life and kept breaking off to sympathize with Jenny and to reminisce, repeatedly forgetting that she was not a niece or other relation of his dead client. She had been wise to accept that the rest of her day was given up to the matter because the silver-haired partner had no pressing business and was bent on spinning out this session.

Mallory rang for a typist to bring cups of tea. He and Jenny had enjoyed one on her arrival but a lot of talk had gone on since then and he felt it time he offered another. While they drank Mallory dropped the subject of Mrs Pendle and asked about the fire in Benfield wood. Jenny told him what she knew. The fire officer had been ready to blame a carelessly discarded cigarette. There had been a number of fires on open land because weeks without rain had turned vegetation to tinder. A match or cigarette which would normally be harmless could easily start a big fire.

'Did you hear anything about the young woman?' asked Mallory spooning extra sugar into his cup.

Jenny looked blank. He said: 'There was a young woman attacked in Ayot wood last night. That's not far from Benfield, is it?'

She told him it was at Ayot crossroads and pressed for

details. Mallory called the young woman who had made the tea and she passed on what she had picked up at lunchtime. They all said how dreadful it was, especially with the man who killed Mary Cross still on the loose. Then the typist went back to her leases and Mallory and Jenny discussed how they could trace Mrs Pendle's scattered relations.

Before leaving town Jenny made an appointment to have her car serviced on Tuesday the following week. Garage staff were on holiday so it could not be done any sooner. With the engine behaving rather badly she began the homeward journey, meaning to call at Ayot St Martin on her way and ask the woman who had made the curtains whether she would consider doing some more.

Near Ayot crossroads she was stopped by the police. In return for her answers to his questions a young detective she knew expanded the story Mallory and his typist had told. A student called Susan Dawlish had staggered up to Meadow Cottage on Sunday evening with blood streaking her face and said she had been attacked in Ayot wood. The Jarmans, who lived there, called Dr Bourton who sent for an ambulance. By the time it reached St Albans hospital Susan had lost consciousness.

The attack was the talk of Ayot St Martin. Before getting in a word about curtains, Jenny heard an elaborate local version of what the constable had said. Susan Dawlish shared a cottage beyond Ayot St Martin. Her friends had gone away for the weekend but she stayed to study. She was a diffident girl known to very few local people because she had lived there only three weeks.

When Jenny reached home Adam was out and had left a message saying he had gone to see a man from Ayot St Martin who had been taken into a geriatric hospital. He had recently stopped visiting the place because a Benfield patient had died there but now the weekly visits had to resume. His note made a mild joke about it.

Jenny put the kettle on because there was no indication that Miles had made himself tea and she felt neglectful. Just because he was withdrawing from the Kings was no reason for them to be less attentive to him. He had seemed even quieter than usual that morning and surprisingly uncurious about the fire. In fact, she had grown disappointed at his lack of interest and found herself exaggerating, saying that if the wind had changed direction the vicarage and St John's would have been engulfed.

Fortunately, she had prevented herself spelling out that his precious carvings might have been lost, a temptation which presented itself because he was obviously more attached to those pieces of stone than to any of the people of Benfield. Jenny could never understand people who rated things more highly than human beings.

When she carried the tea over she coupled her apology for its lateness with a rundown of the day's dramas: Mrs Pendle had died and a girl had been attacked in Ayot wood. Miles listened dispassionately, his grey eyes steady over the rim of her best mug, the one she had alloted him as a friendly gesture when he arrived in Benfield.

After finishing work he left the mug on the draining board in the kitchen and went to the cloakroom to wash as usual. But instead of going away he opened the door of the Kings' sitting room.

Jenny jerked round, surprised. She had frequently asked him in but he had rarely accepted and now, without a knock, there he was. She had slumped in the armchair. The Kings did not have much furniture and were waiting until the decoration of the house was complete before buying more. There was one other comfortable chair in the room but the new curtains were piled on it. She got up to turn the television news off so Miles could talk. He stopped her. He wished to see the news, he said, because there might be something about the Benfield fire.

He drew up a hard chair and sat stiffly alongside but not close to her. After the news he thanked her and disappeared for the night. Jenny was sorry he had been disappointed. No mention had been made of their fire because a more disastrous one had raged in the Chiltern Hills. There had, though, been an item about Susan Dawlish and the police had made guarded suggestions of similarities between this attack and the murder of Mary Cross. They repeated their appeal for information about a man with brown hair and beard.

13

During Monday afternoon something strange happened which set Pauline Williams's mind on a fresh track. A woman called Sandra Sutton telephoned and asked to speak to Dale. He was out and Pauline was away from her desk. The press officer took the call.

Ralph Gough did not mention it to Pauline as he wanted the fun of telling Dale himself. Pauline walked in as Gough was laughing and saying: 'God knows what she thinks *Pinboard* is, Roger. *Pinup*, maybe? Anyway, the lassie claims you run a model agency and you're going to whisk her away from our production line and make her rich and famous!'

Dale shared the easy laughter and explained the business away with the story that he'd had a muddled conversation with the girl while at the factory the previous week. He gave the impression she was rather stupid.

But the incident jogged Pauline's memory and she grew convinced that an extraordinary telephone call months earlier from a girl in another of Brigges's factories amounted to much the same thing. One confused conversation between Roger Dale and a factory girl could be laughed off but two were an improbable coincidence. Pauline remembered something else: the girl who made the first call did not mention a model agency but believed Dale edited a magazine for which she was going to model.

Marion Knox thought nothing of it when Pauline borrowed the press office copy of the *Writers' and Artists' Yearbook*. Dale was busy designing a page for *Pinboard* and paid no attention to what she was up to. Neither of them realized she was reading through the entries for UK publications, taking a special interest in the names of editors and the addresses from which magazines were published.

As the list was alphabetical it did not take long to discover *Angles*, published at 14 High Street, Hertfield, and edited by R. Dales. She copied the information into her diary. Then she went through the rest of the list in case there was anything to confirm or diminish her interest in *Angles*. And all the time she believed she had found the answer and what she was doing was an exercise in delay, that the crucial moment had come for her to ring the police.

She had made a note of the number earlier that day after reading the latest stories about Benfield. The papers had enthusiastically coupled the attack on Susan Dawlish with the murder of Mary Cross. Under such headlines as Has Mary's Killer Struck Again? reporters set out to prove he had. One discovered the vicar's wife was teaching local women self defence and, although her classes predated the murder by many months, chose to call them a 'panic measure to protect women from the demon who roams the district'.

There were photographs of the hospital where Susan Dawlish was unconscious and 'fighting for her life'. Details of that life had been ferreted out or invented where ferreting failed. Susan was presented as a serious, hard-working student whose only close male friend lived in her home town of Southend-on-Sea in Essex. She had fought off her attacker and her 'tremendous will to survive' helped her 'stagger hundreds of yards for help before collapsing'.

Roger Dale continued to ignore his secretary, thinking she looked sulky. She had not joined in the laughter at Ralph Gough's story which just went to show what a dull and puritanical person she was. Jealous, he supposed, of any woman who was pretty enough to be asked to model. When she went out of the room to return a book to the press office he noticed with distaste her heavy legs and regretted once more his bad luck in being stuck with her.

Pauline did not make her call that afternoon. She decided to watch the television news that evening before committing herself because it was possible there had been an arrest. She wished she could talk it over with her flatmate but it was not her day for visiting the hospital. She settled down for a 'quiet' evening with a travel book and with music from the people in the flat overhead, her downstairs neighbours' children romping in the garden, and her windows wide to let in the air and the sounds of central London.

Dale had left the office soon after her and gone to Hertfield. He was annoyed with Sandra Sutton but thought he had talked his way out of the situation with some skill. All he had to do now was keep Sandra quiet. He put some prints into an envelope, added a photocopied list of model agencies and dropped it into a post box with a first-class stamp. And that, he trusted, would be the end of her.

She had been a mistake but not a very damaging one, not the type to cost him his job, get *Angles* into court and send Sheila and the children dashing home to her parents. Confidence about handling Sandra was matched by the growing certainty that the police would now lose interest in his presence at the scene of the murder. Someone had attacked another woman in the same area and they could not possibly connect him with that.

14

Veronica Long believed that most Americans were rich and all were enamoured of English complexions. She dressed in her finest to go to the vicarage and help with the tea for the Arthur Bellerman Society. Once there her behaviour ensured she was not overlooked.

Veronica had only ever had one ambition in her uneventful life: to get away from Benfield. It was not something that could be done through the world of work because her world was the one without it. There could be no falling in love behind the filing cabinets or in the canteen and so she had to seize what chances she had of meeting men. In an old-fashioned way, which she confused with modern realism, Veronica was looking for a man to save her.

She did not entirely lack men and the local man she met secretly in Benfield wood talked constantly of divorcing his wife and marrying her. Veronica was too wise to believe a word of it and now that their trysting place had burned down she expected even less pleasure from the relationship.

'What are these Arthurs like?' she had asked in a guileless way, adopting Jenny King's way of referring to the society members. Jenny replied that the party would be mainly men, teachers or others with a special interest in natural history. Veronica had immediately offered her services for Tuesday afternoon.

She was very fond of Jenny, regarded her as a friend, but when Jenny bounced through the door in Church Cottages on Monday morning, Veronica was afraid she had come to coax her to rejoin the self-defence class. Jenny had always been enthusiastic but since the murder had become evangelistic. Veronica knew she had not been forgiven for dropping out and was relieved when Jenny mentioned the vicarage tea instead.

The Arthurs trailed into St John's while Veronica was in the vicarage kitchen. She was downcast. They did not look rich nor did they look American in the way she expected, which was hung about with cameras and clad in loud check jackets. Actually, she went so far as to doubt whether they were the Arthurs. Her mother told her to stop staring and fill a kettle.

When the men came in for tea Veronica was able, under the guise of handing round mince pies, to scrutinize them more objectively. Several were grey- or white-haired and plainly would not do. She had no prejudice against an *older* man, but an *old* one was definitely not acceptable.

At the other end of the scale were two men she calculated to be in their thirties. A *little* old, maybe, but not a serious impediment. She made sure they got their cups of tea first so she could take a thorough look at them and return later with refills. People served last might not have time for refills.

In her brightest manner Veronica asked the first of the younger men whether he had not thought St John's beautiful, and the Arthur Bellerman memorial beautiful and Benfield beautiful. He said yes, yes, yes. She had expected him to take up a strand and make a conversation of it but all she got in the succeeding minutes were more yeses and one no. Veronica maintained her smile and went to the other man.

Here she did better. He complimented her on the English mince pies and asked whether she had made them herself. Because her whole future hung on mince pies she told a lie. He asked whether she lived in Benfield, whether she did not just love the place, whether St John's was not the prettiest church in Hertfordshire, whether she was not proud to come from the same village as Arthur Bellerman and whether she had ever looked at the flora.

It was her turn for a series of yeses and a no. Bobbing back and forth – trying to look pretty, efficient, full of personality and tragically interesting – Veronica picked up the conversation again. Seeing the flora, she confided, was one of the things she had set her heart on. (She believed it was in the library of an American university because she had once heard that all important English papers were kept in American universities.)

The man said the flora was kept in London. But, he said, there was a rather good facsimile for sale. The Arthur Bellerman Society had published it to commemorate a centenary or a bicentenary, Veronica did not catch which. The not catching did not matter because the man went straight on to say he had his copy with him, outside in the minibus.

Veronica felt the right response was an opening of the eyes, an 'ooo' with the lips and a general conveying that she would drop everything, scones included, to be allowed a few minutes with the flora and, of course, the youngish man.

He was less precipitate. 'I'll show you presently, if you'd really like that.'

They made a plan and they made it in the nick of time because the Reverend Adam King descended like an avenging angel and sent Veronica into the kitchen to fetch more tea. He had become increasingly irritated by the girl's flirting, especially as it was being done at his expense. Jenny had made it a condition that the cost of hiring Mrs Long and Veronica for the scones and the afternoon was to be borne out of his pocket and not her housekeeping.

'We can't begrudge the Arthurs the price of a tea,' he had objected. 'Besides, they're bound to put a hefty donation in the church-repair fund.'

'Pay up,' Jenny had threatened, 'or I'll break into the repair fund for reimbursement.'

So King shooed Veronica away and made a few gaffes about Arthur Bellerman. He was fractious because Jenny had not yet kept her promise and come from the village hall. When she finally did, she dazzled them. She ran across the lawn, a vigorous, brightly dressed figure with a happy laugh and a charming smile. The Arthurs were in love with her before she came through the french window.

Veronica felt upstaged. It did not matter what she did now, Jenny had stolen the show. Jenny was even talking – no, *listening*, which was worse – to the man with the facsimile.

But all was well. Her heart gladdened. He was talking about *her*. Something about her being a lovely young English maiden. Oh dear – something about Veronica's wonderful mince pies. Jenny laughed again but did not spoil things with the truth. Veronica gathered up some used plates and took them to the kitchen.

She ought to have started washing up but she refused to meet the facsimile man while smelling of suds. They had arranged to meet in the church by the memorial and she thought of a clever way not to attract attention when she walked over there. She poured the remains of the tea into a mug, topped it up with hot water because it was stewed, and carried it to St John's for Jeffrey Miles.

Miles was not on his platform. He was near the Arthur Bellerman memorial and for a second, until her eyes grew used to the change of light, Veronica thought he was her American.

'I thought you were one of the Arthurs,' she said chattily. 'Who?'

She told him what she meant, that it was a short form Jenny had for the society and now everyone referred to them that way. He listened without comment and accepted the tea. He did not like it and after a couple of sips set the mug down in a pew. Veronica was still there and he did not like that, either.

He had come down to stretch his legs and see what it was about the memorial that so enthused the group of men. They had found special significance in the wording, something which the vicar confessed to them had escaped his attention and which Miles, overhearing part of the excited conversation, could not grasp. Also, he had come down because he wanted to think. Now Veronica had interrupted.

Altogether he was having a bad day. Work was not going fast enough on the new panel he was uncovering, he could still not make out the subject; people had been in and out of the church disturbing him; and while mounting the ladder he had slipped and scratched the grazed part of his arm. Worse, he had done nothing about creating a new camp. He needed to think hard about the camp and decide whether it was truly worth the effort or whether he might not just as well stay in the bell loft. It no longer entered his head that he might take a room somewhere.

He grew uneasy that Veronica showed no sign of leaving. She was rambling on about the Arthurs. She told him what they had eaten for tea and offered to fetch him a leftover mince pie if he liked. He told her not to bother. Then she asked various things about the flora. This surprised him as she claimed to have spent such a jolly time hearing about it from the Arthurs. He answered her as fully as he could, part of it new knowledge picked up during the Arthurs' discussion in the church.

Unfortunately, Veronica revealed a genuine interest in his replies and finally volunteered that she deeply admired his knowledge of so many interesting things. Miles thought it high time he was back at his carvings and ignoring her but she did not make escape easy. He had to be rather brusque.

Once on the platform he expected her to go away. He craved to be left alone but she was cruelly unaware. She prowled the aisle remarking on everything that caught her eye, their initial conversation freeing her to call across to him. His annoyance increased. Her voice came from one place after another. She was everywhere. She was surrounding him with her presence. His hand gripped his tools more tightly and he tried to apply his mind to the carving, to shut out the prattling girl.

In his head her voice was translated into another voice, that of the woman who had forced herself on him at the last place he had lived. Veronica's laugh became *her* laugh when she had come across him by accident, which was no accident, and kissed him in greeting and never known how he screamed inside at her touch. And Veronica's presence below became *her* presence on the horrifying day she tracked him to Benfield. Instinctively he crouched out of sight, as he had crouched then. But Veronica did not go away as the woman had done. Veronica knew he was up above and she carried on talking to him.

Footsteps sounded on the path outside and she stopped mid-word and looked expectantly at the door but Miles missed that and no one entered. Veronica's voice separated from that other voice and pierced and invaded him until he was coerced into replies. Terse, uncooperative replies.

All of a sudden she shot him a question that was nothing to do with the Dornayes, Arthur Bellerman, the village fallen or church architecture. 'Where are you living?' she asked.

Miles hedged. 'Why?'

She was sitting on the table by the visitors' book, swinging her tanned legs. She giggled. Miles lowered his hands from the carving and looked down at her. 'Why?' he repeated. His grave eyes met hers and she giggled again.

He hated that. A suspicion rose in his mind and his palms became sweaty. Veronica had been in the wood with a man. Miles guessed they had not noticed the camp but suppose he was wrong?

Veronica adjusted the plunging neckline of her dress. She thought that from where he was Jeffrey Miles might be able to see her breasts. She did not mind that. She said: 'Because I'm nosy.'

Miles ought to have turned back to his work and left it at that with her teasing explanation the last word on the subject. But he felt he needed to say something that would put her off. He did not know what and while he wondered about it she spoke again.

'You come and go like magic. I can see the bus stop opposite the vicarage from my bedroom window and I've never seen you near it. For all I know you sleep in here.' She cocked her head at the pews. 'It would be quite comfortable, I suppose. A bit narrow but plenty of length.'

'I don't sleep in a pew.'

Veronica was enjoying her nonsense. He was giving her all his attention and although he was not yet joking with her she expected he would soon. She said: 'All right, then, Jeff. If you're not in the church you must be camping in the wood.' A funny idea struck her and she gave a yelp of laughter. 'I'll bet it was you rubbing two sticks together for a camp fire who set the place alight!'

Miles found himself crossing the platform, felt the rungs of the ladder beneath his feet. Veronica was laughing. Her laughter bounced from the beams, echoed off the walls, filled his head. He got near to her but she twisted away before she could see the expression on his face.

Something had distracted her. Her laughter was cut off. The church door opened and a man stood there with a book in his hand. Veronica hopped off the table and went to him. They sat outside in the sun and forgot Jeffrey Miles among the shadows of St John's.

Miles was desperately worried by what the girl had said and regretted not mentioning Harpury and the bus stop at Ayot crossroads. They were plausible explanations for his 'magic' but she had slipped beneath his guard. Veronica had virtually admitted spying on him. This idea festered long after he resumed work and he deduced the way her curiosity had developed. It had been aroused because he did not use the bus stop near her home, then she had discovered the camp in the wood and noticed, while poking around in the church, that his bag was with him. The Kings had not spotted any of these clues. If they had done they might have reached the same conclusion once the wood burned: he must be sleeping in the church.

Miles feared his response confirmed Veronica's belief and it was inconceivable that she would not tell Jenny. He would be compelled either to move back into the vicarage or else to take a room with some other busybody in Benfield. Otherwise he would have to face the unthinkable: go away and never see his carvings again.

He kept watch on the vicarage, assessing whether Jenny was there or not. He knew Veronica would not readily gossip to King. When it seemed Jenny was out, Miles had a glimmer of hope, then an idea. Blackmail Veronica. He could buy her silence by threatening to tell Jenny what she had been up to in the wood on Saturday evening.

In truth the idea of mentioning such a thing was repellent to him but Veronica was not to know that. The disadvantage was that he would have to approach Veronica and once he had made his point they would be locked together as firmly as any two people who knew each other's secrets.

Mrs Long finished her work at the vicarage and went home

to get supper for her other two daughters. Veronica stayed until the Arthurs left and then washed up. She chattered to the vicar about a facsimile of the flora she had been shown and her interest startled and pleased him. He sat in the kitchen, listening to her while she worked, and thinking he could not remember her previously exhibiting such enthusiasm for anything unconnected with fashion or make-up.

Veronica was still there when Jenny came home. She stayed much later than any of them expected because the conversation moved to self defence. Jenny declared every woman's right to walk where she chose at any time of day or night and her husband argued that, with one girl attacked in Ayot wood and another killed near Hertfield, this was a principle to be tempered with caution. That, said Jenny, was why she was so keen on her class. She convinced Veronica that she should rejoin it the following week.

Veronica eventually left the house but she and Jenny stood outside talking. There was a fresh topic that Veronica had avoided raising in front of the vicar. She knew she could trust Jenny. When the church clock chimed she became guiltily aware of the time and ran off. She did not go the longer way round by road. She raced across the vicarage garden and into the wood. She was never seen again.

15

By Wednesday morning it was plain that Veronica was missing. She had not spent the night with a friend nor made any other haphazard arrangement she had not bothered to tell her mother about. And she had probably planned to meet a man on Tuesday evening. That much appeared clear.

Mrs Long, wringing her hands in the vicarage kitchen, explained that Veronica had always been a bit of a problem. Twice before she had run off. Once she was away for a week and another time longer, both escapades taking place during school holidays. Mrs Long was certain Veronica had done it again.

Until the careworn mother went home, her badly permed hair bobbing out of sight down the vicarage drive, neither of the Kings admitted to any other opinion. Then the vicar blamed Jenny for keeping the girl talking the previous evening and Jenny protested that she had done nothing of the sort.

She decided to tell him. 'She wanted to say something she couldn't in front of you. She hung around waiting for a chance.'

'And what was so important she had to hang around so long?' Veronica's stay had made his supper late.

Jenny said in a careful tone: 'She's looking for work and wanted my advice.' Another time, she thought, Adam would have made a joke about he being the one who was paid to give advice in Benfield. Today he was tetchy. He said nothing. She took a deep breath, knowing he would not like what was coming. 'Veronica wants to be a model.'

'What?' He had an awful premonition that Jenny's attitude had been to back her up.

She said rapidly: 'Yes, I know. She won't make it. But at least she's trying to do something for herself.'

He clapped a hand to his prominent forehead. 'Of all the crack-brained . . .'

'No, it isn't. We talked it through. She's done work for a photographer before, someone she met when she was working at the factory. She's decided to see whether she can get some more and she's written to advertisers.'

His voice was louder than he intended. 'Do you realize what sort of people have to advertise for girls?'

'Yes, and so does Veronica. We talked about that too. She says she's been very careful not to write to any that sound dubious.'

'If you ask me the whole business is extremely dubious.'

She raised her voice to match his. 'Well, she didn't ask you and she didn't ask me until she'd done it. What was I supposed to do? Give her a lecture on moral standards and send her home in disgrace?'

He said through gritted teeth that it would have been wiser. Jenny swept on to say that Veronica had not yet received replies to her letters because she had given a friend's address as she did not want her mother to know about it. 'She was talking about going up to London today and collecting any replies. Her friend isn't on the telephone.'

She saw from Adam's face that it would be best to keep to herself Veronica's other revelation: the same friend had given her the copy of *Angles* which her mother had confiscated.

She said lamely: 'Perhaps she caught the bus last night or early this morning.'

Adam had darker ideas. He did not voice them. He said: 'She was behaving very badly yesterday. I don't think she should have turned up here dressed the way she was.'

'Well, there you are. The dress wasn't suitable for an afternoon serving tea at a vicarage. Doesn't that show she had plans to go somewhere after it? London, perhaps?'

'Wouldn't she have told you? She seems to have told you everything else.'

She shrugged. He said: 'If you'd seen the way she was flirting with that Arthur, the chap with the facsimile flora . . .' He remembered Veronica's eager cheerfulness and her surprising degree of interest when she had talked about the flora over the washing up. It crossed his mind that perhaps there was something between Veronica and that man.

He tried to explain but gave up, thinking that the Arthurs were in London as well as Veronica's obliging friend and if the girl became a police matter he would have to report her behaviour at the vicarage. In the meantime he found it easier to repeat his challenge to Jenny's easy acceptance that a jobless, unqualified girl with nothing but a sweet face and a shapely body might try to make her living as a model. He did not consider himself a prude but thought modern society had gone far enough without vicars' wives conniving at that type of thing. Jenny's assertion that the effort represented a long-awaited chink in Veronica's apathy did not sway him.

They were cut off by Jeffrey Miles appearing beside them with a request for a cup of coffee. Penitent at having forgotten him, Jenny went to pains to make him welcome. Then, when he retreated to the church, she announced she had to go to Pendle Cottage on an errand for Mallory, the solicitor. The piece of business was not half as urgent as she made it sound but she needed to escape before trouble brewed again. Adam grumbled but she left all the same.

There were bluebells on the bank, birds in holly hedges. Back Lane was a haven. She let herself into the cottage. The job she had pretended important was to clear out perishables. Butter and cheese were in the fridge, an unopened carton of milk and a nearly finished one. She thought she might take home the new milk, because she was a bit short after the Arthurs' tea, and give away the other useful things. But her mind was not really on any of this.

She had a mental picture of a happy, laughing, exalted Veronica, Veronica as she had last seen her. A dreadful fear flooded her body. She slammed the fridge door.

In the back sitting room she dropped on to the chair she had used all those times she visited Mrs Pendle, Ada Pendle, although she had never progressed to the Ada stage. For the first time since her friend died Jenny knew tears. She and Mrs Pendle had not been related by blood but there were other things that tied people. They had shared what was in their hearts and that was a stronger bond.

She dried her eyes, reminding herself how Mrs Pendle would have mocked anyone being maudlin. Mrs Pendle had got her wish: she had died in her own home and done it before her faculties had deteriorated. Even after death a certain dignity would attach to her as Jenny had discovered when Mallory told her the funeral arrangements.

The air had grown heavy. Jenny's head ached and she felt increasingly depressed. She brooded that Adam was being unfair to her, that he frequently was, and that regardless of common sense he believed his vocation made his judgement invariably superior to hers. Yet Benfield had responded to her. She was happy there and able to do things to strengthen the community. It would be a bitter paradox, she thought, if her commitment to the parishioners were to damage her marriage.

She would have been crosser had she known that immediately she drove away Adam had passed on to Mrs Long most of what she had shared with him. He had persuaded the woman to let him telephone the police and report Veronica missing. Mrs Long was grateful to him and, as he had anticipated, did not complain that the information had been withheld until then. It never pleased him that Jenny was always held to be above criticism while he was not.

Jenny arrived home to an empty house. Her instinct was to look for him, say something to take the sting from her earlier anger because she had begun to look for excuses for him. Perhaps he was unwell? He had been difficult to live with for the past few days, in marked contrast to his mood a few weeks back when he had been bubbling with enthusiasm, especially about his carvings. He hardly mentioned them now. She went up the path between the lichened stones and let herself into the church, very softly.

Jeffrey Miles did not stir. He was crouching by the central panel, hands moving over the hideous serpent. Caressing it, Jenny thought, and the word troubled her because it suggested a personal warmth he had never shown.

She put her trust in the healing atmosphere of St John's

even if this proved yet another of the increasingly common times when she was unable to pray. Before she began to meditate she noticed a full and forgotten mug of tea on the wood of the neighbouring pew. Then she sat, careless of the time and, until she rose, careless of Jeffrey Miles watching her.

16

The name Veronica Long hit Pauline Williams with the shock of familiarity. That was the name of the girl who had written to Roger Dale offering her services as a photographic model!

Marion Knox burst into Pauline's room with Wednesday morning's paper in her hand. 'It's the same name, isn't it? It *must* be the same girl.' Ruth James herself could not have been more theatrical. 'All these things are happening along the road Roger uses and he fits the description of the man the police want. Honestly, Pauline, I think you ought to say something.'

'What about you?' Pauline asked. 'Or are you as wary as I am of wasting the time of the police with a series of jumped-to conclusions?'

'No!' Marion cried. 'But you know more about it than I do. I can't tell them what his movements were at the relevant times and I'm not the one who opened the letter.'

'What was the address?'

'What?' Marion was slowed by the question.

'If the letter bore a Benfield address we'd have noticed. Any Hertfordshire address would have registered because that's where Roger lives.'

Marion said she had no idea about the address, she had been more interested in the contents of the letter. Pauline told her she was positive it was London but did not explain that she had put the letter in a new envelope without a stamp so Dale would assume it had been dropped through the door. Without a London address that would not have been credible.

'Oh, Pauline,' wailed Marion, reluctantly leaving for her

own office as Ralph Gough arrived for work, 'if only you hadn't thrown that letter away!'

Pauline totted up the evidence against Dale, aware of his children's faces smiling at her from his desk as she did so. There was nothing conclusive to link him with either the Cross or Dawlish case and coincidence could dispose of two Veronica Longs and two editors with similar names. The most damning thing was his resemblance to the photofit picture, but the police had questioned him and not detained him.

A new situation was arising which made her ultra sensitive to any buried desire for revenge. The revolt on the sixth floor had resulted in a change of directors and the man now at the end of Dale's reporting line had raised difficulties about *Pinboard*. Dale had not acted on instructions and had then lied, claiming that messages had never been passed to him and letting Pauline carry the blame.

Although she could not bring herself to ring the police she telephoned *Angles*. Dale was not in the *Pinboard* office and she wondered whether he could be there. If he answered, some of her suspicions would be confirmed. If a stranger did, an edifice of speculation would collapse.

She got an answering machine. The message was not in Dale's voice and the man did not give his name. Her attempt to check had failed and before she could think of another way Dale appeared.

In the middle of the afternoon, when he had been summoned to a meeting, the door of the room swung open and a short plump blonde with a baby face walked in and said she was Sandra Sutton and, please, where was Roger Dale? Oblivious of the effect she was having on Pauline, Sandra described how she had been writing to model agencies for some while and that day visited one in the West End. The very nice people there had given her good tips about getting into the modelling game.

Pauline supposed one of the tips was to lose weight. She kept an interested expression on her face and let Sandra rattle on. At last she stopped talking about the very nice people and arrived at the reason she wanted Dale. 'They asked me to get some photos taken and I said I'd done that and would post them. I don't know whether he'd keep them here.' She looked doubtfully around the *Pinboard* office. There was not so much as a rude calendar since Pauline had asked Dale to take it down.

'Probably not,' murmured Pauline, daring herself to put the impertinent questions which would reveal the extent of Dale's involvement with Sandra Sutton and modelling.

Before she managed more than a gentle prod in that direction Dale walked in. He'd had a bad time at his meeting. His stories about Pauline's negligence had not been swallowed and he was going to have to work hard to repair the damage.

His face switched from annoyance to forced welcome as he saw Sandra. She started to tell him how much she needed the photographs he had taken but he grabbed her arm and hustled her out into the corridor. Over his shoulder he told Pauline he would not be back that day. The overlords on the sixth floor would have to wait, placating them was no longer his priority. The essential thing was to get Sandra Sutton away, fast.

There was only one place he could take her. The *Angles* office. He tried convincing her that prints were in the post but she ought to have received them in the first delivery that day. Rather than risk her telephoning *Pinboard* and grumbling that they were lost, he would give her some more. After that he would drive her to a Hertfordshire station where he could put her on a train north.

Sandra did not demur. She was brimming with pleasure at the compliments the men at the West End agency had paid her. Only later would it penetrate that they had been kindly putting her off.

Dale explained the trip to Hertfield by saying he wanted her to meet his partner, although he was actually depending on the fact that Lomax would not be there. 'He runs the agency,' he said, preparing his way out for the inevitable time when he needed it. Sandra Sutton had already proved far more of a nuisance than he dreamed when he spotted that ripe little figure in the factory.

Before they reached Hertfield the police waved the car down. Mary Cross's face stared from a poster while they took Dale's name and address and so on. They were not officers he had spoken to before but it made no difference. The computer would recognize him all right. 'Another entry for Roger Dale . . . This time he had a young girl with him . . .'

The man with the clipboard moved to Sandra's window. Name? Address? The pen skimmed the page. Dale held his breath, praying Sandra would use discretion.

She did not. 'I'm a model,' she said, trying out a refined accent.

'Oh yes, miss. And how old are you, if you don't mind my asking?' The sergeant looked into her baby face as she told him the truth. He gave Dale a long look before letting him drive on.

As they moved off Sandra roared with laughter and gave Dale a smile wreathed with complicity. He was beginning to hate her.

Al Lomax was no keener. He had gone to the *Angles* office to calculate how much money he could ask from Roger Dale to buy him out. There were other matters to resolve before he said yes to a share in Rex's dog but everything hinged on whether he could scratch together the asking price.

'What's she doing here?' Lomax said, his voice tight with accusation.

Sandra found him very rude, especially as he was presumably the man who ran the model agency. He did not even say hello to her. In the West End the men had been friendly but this one seemed unlikely to pay her any compliments.

Dale pushed by into the darkroom, afraid of finding more torn prints. Lomax had not touched the new ones. As his gesture had been ineffective, he had decided to have it out with Dale and insist that ugly pictures of unattractive teenagers were banned. The situation did not entirely displease him. Their agreement prevented him snatching his money back but he could not be expected to let his name be associated with a magazine which had sunk to illegal depths. Dale's behaviour was providing an excellent excuse for Lomax to withdraw from *Angles*.

He followed Dale into the darkroom. 'I asked what she's doing here,' he hissed. 'I do recognize her, you know, even from your rotten photographs.'

Dale was selecting prints. 'She wants these,' he said matching Lomax's tone. 'Then I'm putting her on a train home to Manchester. OK?'

'No,' said Lomax. 'I'm putting that bit of jailbait on the train home. That way I can make sure she goes and understands she's to stay there.'

Lomax was deadly serious. Dale shrugged: 'Please yourself, Al.' He had no choice but to run the risk that Sandra would expose the deception about the model agency. He took the prints to her, riffled through them allowing her no time to look at them properly, handed them over in an envelope and said: 'Change of plan. Al will take you to the station.'

Her face clouded. She did not approve of this. Lomax picked up his car keys. 'Come on,' he said, the first words he had addressed to her. And he said to Dale: 'When I get back, Roger, we'll talk.'

Dale smarted. Lomax's car glided away taking Sandra Sutton out of his life.

17

Once he had put Sandra Sutton on the train north, Al Lomax made two telephone calls. The first elicited that there was to be a dog fight that evening and the second gave the news to Roger Dale.

Lomax's determination to challenge Dale about the standard of *Angles* was evaporating. He had thought of an alternative plan to getting Dale to buy him out and it was in his interests not to upset things too much. With luck he could persuade Dale to sell the magazine altogether and share in the purchase of a terrier.

He had reservations about Havoc because there was only Rex's word for its pedigree. No one said Rex was lying but Lomax had noticed people were scared of Rex's temper and careful not to cross him. He reasoned that if the pup had the potential Rex claimed, buyers would be queueing. Instead, Rex was pushing for a sale.

He made his call to Dale obscure in case there was a crossed line and unexpected guests turned up at the meeting place. Dale understood and said yes, he would be there. Lomax's change of mood was puzzling but the important thing was that Lomax was taking him to a fight. He drove home happier than he had been for days.

Monday had been bad because he had a hangover and Sheila had scarcely spoken to him. Things had not improved much on Tuesday. At work on Wednesday he reaped the result of his deceptions but Wednesday evening was going to be all right. His luck had turned.

Sheila was withdrawn and sighed heavily when he said he was going out again. She served supper but ate little herself.

Her left wrist was bandaged where she had cut it on the broken glass on Sunday. She did not explain whether the injury was intentional or genuine accident and would talk about only the murder, relating the latest rumours. After Sunday's scene she avoided asking him to stay with her or protesting when he did not.

Mrs Catesby had taken Sheila to hospital on Sunday to have her wound stitched and Mrs Catesby had recommended a company to replace the damaged french window with a new unit. This would be stronger, safer, and, of course, much more expensive than putting in a new pane of glass. Sheila had placed an order and told her husband on Monday evening.

Dale wanted to cancel it but could not face any more hysteria. He tested the temperature on Wednesday with a few remarks but she was unmistakably chilly. Before he could make headway someone came to the door.

'I'm sorry,' said Sheila, springing from the table as though she were responsible for 'Greensleeves' starting up.

Dale heard a man's voice and then the front door closed. Sheila reappeared beside him. 'Police,' she whispered, frightened.

Dale fought down several kinds of reaction. His face assumed a blankness, the personality shut away deep behind his eyes. 'Well, what do they want?' He was proud of the calm voice.

Sheila flung her hands wide. 'How do I know? They asked for you. I'm sorry, that's all I know. They want you.'

Dale made the brief journey to the sitting room where the police waited. A road check, that's what he had always imagined. One day there would be a road check at which they did not wave him on. What he had never expected was that they would appear in Harpury.

Imagination was notoriously lazy about facts, he thought as he went along the hall. There was no reason why the police should not go to his home. He had given them the address frequently enough. But thank God they had come when Caroline and Timothy were in bed.

He reached the sitting-room door without having made up

his mind what to say when they asked why he had lied about his movements the evening Mary Cross died. A lean, sandy-haired young man in a sports jacket was looking down the room at the smashed window. He turned an alert face and introduced himself as Detective Sergeant Travis, his swarthy companion as Detective Constable Ross. After the preliminaries Travis asked whether Dale was the editor of *Angles*. Then the real questions began, questions about the magazine's advertisers.

Dale adopted his most helpful manner, believing he could fob the sergeant off. He could not. Travis asked Dale to take them to the magazine office where the details Dale was not providing would be available.

Dale glanced at the door. He had taken care to close it and did not seriously think Sheila would be listening outside yet he lowered his voice as he said: 'My wife doesn't know about the magazine. I don't want her upset. Why don't you turn your car round while I tell her I'm going out?'

To his relief Travis agreed. Dale heard their car make the necessary three-point turn at the end of the close while he told Sheila the police were looking for a witness to a road accident but as he could not help they had gone. In the same breath he said it was time he left for the appointment he had previously mentioned.

Sheila had no reason not to believe him and loaded the dishwasher while Dale reversed his car from the drive and caught up with the police further down the close. In Hertfield he let them into the office and the tone of the conversation changed. Nobody had to worry about upsetting Sheila, punches need not be pulled.

Dale demanded to know what all this was about. Sergeant Travis said the police had received a complaint from a member of the public about the content of the magazine. His colleague was flicking through back numbers and setting aside those that especially interested him. Most of them.

Travis drew Dale's attention to a couple of advertisements which, he said, anyone in the photography business or publishing might suspect were not as legal, decent and honest as the law demanded. Dale mumbled any excuses he could think of, along the lines that he had not noticed the offending box-number advertisements.

Travis revealed that Jenny King's complaint to Inspector Addison had caused Dale's problems. Addison had passed the magazine to a colleague and Travis had been asked to make inquiries. Before setting out for Harpury he knew that one of the offending advertisements had the same wording as one that used to appear in big-circulation photographic magazines before there was a prosecution followed by a tightening up by advertising sales staff. The other one was written in a different style.

Angles was not the most pornographic magazine Travis had ever seen, and investigating it no compensation for being taken off the murder inquiry, but he knew that Roger Dale's name had cropped up several times during the Mary Cross case. He had made the link with R. Dales, editor of *Angles*, because the greengrocer told him the editor lived in Harpury. Dale was one of many men stopped at road checks because they and their cars looked like the driver and vehicle reported near the body. Travis believed it beyond his luck to trip over the murderer while the rest of the force were drawing blanks but he meant to keep his eyes open.

Dale detested the silence. Travis was reading the subscribers' list. Ross was gathering up magazines and photographs. Then Travis asked, very politely, whether Dale would mind if they took things away. Dale agreed, knowing they could come back with authorization as soon as they liked if he refused.

'It's a pity', said Travis, 'there's nothing to identify the people who placed those two advertisements. If the information comes to light you will let me know, won't you?'

Dale said he would. Travis opened the door and held it for Ross who was laden. When they had gone Dale subsided into the chair behind the desk and wiped a handkerchief over his face. His heart had kept up an erratic clamour ever since he set eyes on Travis and now, when he screwed his eyes tight and buried his face in his hands, he could still see that intelligent young face with the alert blue eyes.

He pulled himself together and looked at his watch. If he

did not hurry he might not be in time to meet Lomax. Despite his urgency he drove gently knowing it would be especially foolish to be caught speeding. All sorts of suspicions would be raised.

The pub was remote. In the car park he recognized vehicles from Sunday. The pub door opened and two of the men came out, then Lomax.

'What kept you?' Lomax asked with a veneer of sarcasm. 'I thought you were keen on this.' He was worried Dale's lateness meant he was not sufficiently keen and the idea of getting him to share the cost of a dog would fail.

Dale got into Lomax's car, apologizing. He remembered using the same words on Sunday so he expanded slightly. 'There's a family crisis. We've mislaid a blue plastic space-man.'

Reassured, Lomax laughed. He wound down the car window to let the breeze cool the interior. On the way he chatted, talking all around the business of acquiring and keeping a terrier without ever telling Dale exactly what was on his mind. He wanted to make it attractive before it became a proposition.

Roger Dale kept silent about the police visit to *Angles*, confident he would be able to conceal it permanently from Lomax. He was more troubled about whether he could hide from Travis that he had placed one of those suspect box-number advertisements himself.

18

Up on the Chiltern scarp the roads wind west into Buckinghamshire and near the county boundary Lomax made a right turn into a skinny lane. More turns, skinnier lanes. Then he was bumping the car across a farmyard. There was something odd about the place.

As farmhouses go it was curiously tidy. Even the horses' heads poking out of stable doors appeared neatly adjusted to hang in perfect line. Four vehicles were already in the yard. Joe, the man who looked like an alderman, was lighting a cigar. Rex greeted Dale with a conspiratorial smile. The men stood in casual knots, giving away the underlying tension by nervous glances in the direction of approaching cars.

When they were all present and sure no one was following uninvited they went to the stables, a Victorian building with a central arch and a cupola. Horses were ranged to one side of the arch and the men were led to the other.

The empty swimming pool inside the stable block was a glamorous creation recalling 1930s' opulence. On its black floor was painted a golden palm tree, its fluid shape cut by lines of adhesive tape marking the fifteen-foot-square ring where the dogs were to fight.

The owner, an ageing pop singer, was swapping jokes as the dogs were brought in, their pungent smell mingling with cigar smoke. Two were dragged to the steps and, when they bounded down into the pool, led to opposite sides of the ring. Bets were made as they snarled, desperate to be freed. The atmosphere in the room quickened.

Chains were slipped, the animals lunged. Cheers soon changed to gibes as men who had expected better form lost money. Two other dogs were brought in. From the video recording Dale recognized the dog Rex claimed as Havoc's sire. As its cavernous jaws opened Dale shut his eyes. The dog facing it was no match at all, a Staffordshire bull terrier lacking the menace to chase a cat.

Dale's head rang with the Staffordshire's screams and the smell of hot blood choked him. When he looked again the smaller dog's jaw had been ripped and the pit's teeth were locked on his ear. Men controlling the fight were intervening but the pit wrenched and the ear was lost.

Its tongue slavered over the blood around its mouth before it renewed the onslaught. Splashes of blood jewelled the golden palm tree.

Amid the hullaboloo Lomax watched the ring with silent intensity and Dale knew he was searching for a similarity between Rex's pup and the beast below them. Men forced it from its prey and the Staffordshire staggered a few steps before crumpling. Blood was pumping over the pale fur of his breast yet he regained his feet and lurched forward. He was growling. He had growled throughout. Except when he was screaming.

A time came when he found a way into the pit's flesh but it was uselessly late. Minutes later, when the excitements of death and triumph were equally exhilarating, Dale discovered how much he was enjoying it. 'Maybe not Havoc,' he told Lomax, 'but you must get a dog.'

'What's wrong with Havoc?' Lomax wondered what Dale knew.

'Nothing, but he hasn't got the evil in his eye that this one has.'

Lomax nodded. He did not know whether the lack of it proved Havoc was not sired by the monster they had just seen in action or whether that look was something which came with the habit of killing.

That evening there were several fights. Sometimes the dogs were evenly matched, sometimes not, but there were always men ready to gamble on outsiders' chances.

Suddenly it stopped. The stable door was thrown open by a shouting lookout. The pop star moved with the speed he used to dodge fans after performances and water was rushing from a hose into the pool. He drenched men ripping tape off the tiles. A pair of dogs was still there, locked by teeth and fur, until a man jabbed a cigar butt into the rectum of one and hauled him away.

The commotion meant a police raid and the pop star's screams meant they were to get out. The last Dale saw of the pool was the painted palm tree shimmering beneath water. A man with a mop was rubbing blood from its gold fronds. Water the colour of Campari swirled down a gilded outlet.

Lomax and Dale did not get into the farmhouse to hide in the cellar with the rest. They were late into the yard and no one told them what to do. Cars were being shunted about. A barn was opened and several were locked inside it. Others took the place of family cars in the garages and family cars were parked close to the locked doors. Dogs were muzzled and shut in the concealed vehicles. Lomax's car was left in the yard. He cursed. Straight down the farm track, through the stable arch, a police car was closing on them.

Dale tugged his sleeve. 'This way, Al.'

They pelted for the trees. Striking away from the house and track, they crouched when they heard the car grow nearer. 'Keep still,' Dale hissed.

They had not gone far. The slam of the car door sounded within hands' reach. Footsteps to the front of the house were frighteningly loud. Dale pressed into the dank smell of crushed bluebells. In future their scent would always bring that moment back to him.

He thanked his luck that it was Lomax's car and not his red Ford parked in full view. Lomax would face any awkward questions. The police could trace his ownership through the computer at the vehicle-licensing department. Dale was not bothered about Lomax's danger. It suited him to have Lomax harried by the police and made jumpy about dog fighting because then Lomax would have to shut up about *Angles*.

They heard the door of the house open, the pop star's voice and then the door closing. There were no more sounds, suggesting the police had been admitted. Lomax and Dale scuttled away. Five minutes later Lomax protested it was pointless going further because they must go back for the car. Dale had no intention of going back but did not say so.

The police car drove off. They heard it halt at the end of the track, then speed down the lane. 'All right,' said Lomax struggling to his feet. He sounded exhausted, physically and mentally. The thrill of the fight followed by the fear of detection had worn him out. 'Let's get the car and clear out of here – *fast.*'

'You go. You can pick me up in the lane,' Dale suggested.

Lomax objected but at last conceded there was no purpose in both of them being caught if any police had lingered at the house. Unhappy but resigned, he started back to the yard.

Dale pushed on, keeping roughly parallel to the farm track and expecting to meet the lane before long. Lomax would not want to hang around for him if he was not where he had promised to be.

The wood was not well managed. There were impenetrable areas to be skirted around. While he was stock still getting his bearings he heard the sound.

Dale's blood pounded. He saw no one but the noise continued. Someone else was moving through the trees. They were on a collision course.

Dale veered to the left, seeking deeper cover while the other person passed. When he stopped after a few yards there was only the gentle noise of foliage he had disturbed. Then the worrying sounds resumed. Closer.

A man broke through the trees. He was a young muscular fellow who darted forward at the sight of Dale. Dale meant to stand his ground but his stomach tightened and he backed up against a tree.

The man stood inches from him, hands loosely clenched. 'This is private property. What do you want here?'

Dale concealed his relief. The man could not be a policeman. He must be one of the lookouts. Even so it did not follow that he would let him go in time to meet Lomax. Dale's voice wavered: 'I was at the house. I mean the swimming pool. I had to leave in a hurry.'

The man's hands grew limp but he did not move. 'So what are you doing here?'

'Making for the lane. A friend is going to pick me up in his car.'

The man thought about that but decided to be satisfied. 'Well, keep going. Over there.' He pointed Dale back on course and watched him go. Twice Dale peered over his shoulder and saw him standing in the same place, making sure he did what he had been told. The third time he looked there was no one there.

He heard the thrum of an engine idling and blundered forward, getting scratched and losing a jacket button before stumbling on to the tarmac. The car was out of sight around a bend. Dale ran for it, willing Lomax to give him the extra seconds he needed. He grasped the door handle and fell into the passenger seat. All Lomax said was: 'You took your time, didn't you?' Then the car was swaying away. They had enough to talk about without mentioning Sandra Sutton or *Angles*.

19

Someone had been into Pendle Cottage. Jenny King was sure of it. The cottage had passed to Mrs Pendle's nephew in Somerset and he had told Mallory he could not visit it until the funeral. Whoever had been in had no right to do so. Jenny and Mallory held keys, no one else.

As soon as she unlocked the door on Thursday morning she felt an intuitive uneasiness. Before she reached the end of the passage she was certain something was wrong.

She turned back. Her eyes settled on a ledge on the wooden panelling by the front door. Mrs Pendle had kept her key there but it was no longer in place. Jenny remembered picking it up off the floor on Monday and putting it on the table by the telephone. It was not on the table either.

She considered the telephone, working out whether she or Dr Bourton had used it last on Monday and recollecting that she had done so herself. Left-handed, she would not normally have replaced the receiver on the cradle in the direction she now found it.

In the kitchen she found confirmation of her suspicions. Food she had come to clear from the fridge had been used. The full carton of milk was open. Things were not on the shelves as she remembered them.

She whisked open cupboard doors but there were no other obvious signs until she looked in the dustbin and saw on top of the rubbish an empty milk carton which had contained an inch or two the previous day. In the sitting room something else came to light. Fingers had trailed through dust on top of the television set. She was absolutely certain it had not been like that on Wednesday.

Jenny darted upstairs and opened the bathroom door. No signs of disturbance. The same yellow towel hung as it had done. The hot water was switched off as she had left it on Monday.

In Mrs Pendle's bedroom everything was exactly as it had been when she found the metal box of papers for Mallory. But in the back room the single bed was mildly crumpled. She turned back the cover. There were no hairs on the white pillow case and the sheet was firmly tucked in. Yet it was obvious someone had lain on the bed.

Proof was now incontrovertible. If Mallory had called he might conceivably have helped himself to a cup of tea and opened fresh milk but he would never have lain down in the back room.

Jenny was indignant that anyone should enter the cottage without permission. It was a private place, a home, the accumulation of possessions which were all that survived of Mrs Pendle. Someone had invaded Jenny's memories.

She had loved Mrs Pendle and was not awkward about using the word. Both were outsiders in Benfield. Neither could identify completely with the people of the village but they had an instant rapport and a deep affection had been quickly established. What they shared was created from conversation and peaceable silences within the walls of Pendle Cottage. This was a place where they had exchanged secrets, sought encouragement and made promises. No one else had been involved and because Mrs Pendle had been increasingly housebound she and Jenny had met nowhere else. Their friendship was born and was broken off in the cottage.

Maybe, thought Jenny, that was why she had acquiesced at Mrs Pendle's wish to stay in her own home instead of moving to what people called sheltered accommodation. Maybe she had not sincerely believed it best for her friend to go on alone. Maybe behind her encouragement there had been the selfish desire to have Mrs Pendle at the cottage and their friendship unending and unchanged.

Yet it had ended and in a brutal way. Awake at nights Jenny pictured Mrs Pendle attempting to telephone for help, the receiver dropping and the woman falling. Jenny imagined her hearing people outside, probably the weekenders, and dragging herself to the door where she collapsed before she could unlock it. Oh yes, the friendship had been ended in the most savage way of all.

Pendle Cottage was of paramount importance to Jenny because it was all she had left. For someone to get in and make themselves at home was more painful than if they had broken into the vicarage. She would hate that too but she and Adam would go on together and there would be more happiness and more secrets. Pendle Cottage violated was irreparably hurtful.

Jenny began to empty the fridge. If the intruder returned, a house without food and drink would be much less attractive. When all the items were on the kitchen table and she was about to pack them in a bag she had a change of heart. She realized she was not taking the things to protect the house. She was doing it to punish the intruder and that was a mean act, especially as she had always meant to give the food away. Quickly, she put everything back into the fridge.

In the evening, she decided, she would come back to the cottage and find out who was there and why. Her heart leaped at the realization that it could be Veronica. Most local people would have heard by now that Mrs Pendle had died but only Veronica had unexpectedly and mysteriously left home.

Buoyed up with this idea Jenny decided to leave everything else untouched rather than frighten the girl away. Camping out in a local cottage was not the most reprehensible thing Veronica could do and if she knew she was discovered she might genuinely run off to London. Benfield had already concluded she had gone there and Jenny had heard a disquieting rumour about Veronica and a married man.

At first when Adam said he had reported Veronica missing, Jenny had been annoyed. As the girl's disappearance stretched into the second day she admitted he was right. Although Mrs Long insisted that her daughter had run off twice before and come to no harm, on those occasions Veronica had telephoned her. This time, not a word.

Jenny's mind went back to the cottage telephone. Veronica was not left-handed. If she had used it she would most naturally have set the receiver down in the way it now faced.

With these comforting facts fitting neatly together, Jenny ran upstairs to close doors she had opened. And it was as she was mounting the stairs this second time that she could see beneath the bed in the back room. Something had been stuffed under it.

On hands and knees she drew it out. All thought of Veronica fled. She was holding a heavy grey bag. Jeffrey Miles's bag.

Bewildered she shoved it back and knelt, a confusion of emotions depriving her of clear thought. All her arguments in favour of letting Veronica stay unmolested at the cottage evaporated. Because it was Jeff, it was different.

She did not understand why it should be different and tried to work out what his presence there meant. Clearly he was not living in Harpury. She gave herself credit for having always found the story hard to swallow. Perhaps he had been living in Hertfield, where she had seen him in the library, and perhaps he had wearied of the journey and impertinently used the cottage.

Her face coloured at another thought. The journey to Hertfield was about three miles so he could not have *wearied*. But Adam was not paying him much and he had taken on the major expense of somewhere to stay. It was inescapable that he had left the vicarage because of her attempts to be friendly, a friendship he utterly rejected.

Gradually Jenny brought herself round to the stage where she was willing to allow Miles to stay at the cottage. Mrs Pendle, she believed, would have approved. She had been very attached to St John's and interested in the uncovering of the carvings. Jenny had promised to take her to see them once work was completed.

Having had Miles for a lodger Jenny felt no qualms about letting him use the cottage. He would not damage it, hold riotous parties or pilfer. He would make the ideal tenant although it was a great shame he had not troubled to ask first.

She mulled it over as she drove to Ayot St Martin on her

next call. No one else knew he was there and she could keep the information to herself until the funeral. Then the nephew would visit it and perhaps stay at the cottage a day or two before telling Mallory whether he wanted it sold. Jenny made up her mind to have a word with the nephew in the hope of formalizing the arrangement Miles had begun so informally. If she went about it tactfully Miles might be allowed to live there until his work was done. In that way she could make it up to him for inadvertently chasing him out of the vicarage.

20

Stan Albury spent Thursday afternoon digging a grave on the western side of the churchyard. The old handyman's rhythmic spadework accompanied Miles's delicate probing of plaster through the heat of the day. When Miles broke off work Albury was still there.

Coming out of the porch, Miles did not see him at first. The light was brillant after the low level indoors and Albury was just clambering out of the hole. He rolled a cigarette, struck a match against a gravestone, and lit up. Miles stood listening to a thrush which had sung prettily and tirelessly for hours. Above Benfield wood rooks were circling and high in a horse chestnut pigeons called. The heart of the wood was burnt out but from the edge there was nothing to indicate this. Miles spotted Albury.

Albury was a wrinkled countryman who boasted of never having been to London. His parochialism extended to disliking people who had no family links with Benfield and it was a persistent rumour that he had given the previous vicar a bad time. The Kings were equally foreign but fared better although it was rash of those who told Albury to his face that this was because he was soft about Jenny King.

The Reverend Adam King was tolerant of Albury's finicky ways and showed he appreciated the value of the old man's experience of St John's and its peculiarities. Albury made it plain he regarded himself as the superior partner in their joint enterprises, a situation King found more amusing than irritating. Few men in the village would have been willing to take on the menial and largely unpleasant tasks and he was prepared to let Albury carry them out until he wanted to stop. It was a pity Albury was blasphemous but that was one of his foibles the vicar had to bear.

Albury detested Jeffrey Miles. The old fellow drew on his cigarette, saw Miles and scowled. Miles nodded an unsmiling greeting. Albury did not move a muscle. When Miles returned from the vicarage, having handed back his tea mug and washed, Albury was in exactly the same stance. He might have been one of the stone monuments if it had not been for the coil of smoke in the summer air.

Miles refused to vary his routine because of Albury and strode up the path towards the narrow gate beyond him. Albury flung his cigarette into the grave as Miles passed and then spat into the grass. Before Miles had taken many more steps he heard the sound of the spade again.

He did not care what Albury thought or what he did. Miles was happy, or as nearly happy as he dared to be. His experience of happiness was slender. He had been happy in his camp in the wood and initially he had been happy at the vicarage. Those spells had not lasted long and neither had earlier ones. The pattern of disappointment was too well established for him to trust that things would go on being all right. Someone would spoil it. Someone always did.

Miles kept close to the perimeter of the wood until he could see Pendle Cottage and be certain no one was there. Convinced, he slithered down the steep bank and opened the gate.

He went straight upstairs to the back bedroom, the room he liked best for its view of fields, a wood near the crossroads and the roofs of Ayot St Martin. He flopped on the bed and gazed over the fields, amused when the Harpury bus pulled up at the stop. If he had truly meant to catch it, he would have missed it.

Miles drew his bag from under the bed and unzipped it. Beneath his sleeping bag and clothes were his camping things. He could have spread himself around, used the cupboards or anything he chose, but he wanted his possessions kept together. If the time came to get out, he could be fast.

His escape route was ready: through the hedge behind the

cottage, into the field and away to one of the lanes although there might be a footpath to the main road. Downstairs in the back sitting room he consulted a map on the wall. Mrs Pendle had been one of those people who own too much furniture and too many things for the space in which they live. Paintings and other framed items clustered on the walls. Miles knew from Jenny's conversation that Mrs Pendle had moved to the cottage in old age and he presumed she had moved from a much bigger house. He needed a couple of attempts to find the map he had previously spotted.

It was a very old print of Benfield, so old it was spelled Benefield and Hertfordshire was written in a curious way too. He did not know whether that was ignorance or affectation on the part of the printmaker because the spelling of place names showed no consistency. However, Back Lane was marked although not named as the map covered too big an area for that type of detail.

A dot indicated only one building and in the wrong position to be Pendle Cottage. Miles was positive there was nothing now on that stretch of road. Near the dot was marked a footpath crossing fields to Ayot crossroads.

Satisfied, he went to the bedroom window and strained to see signs of a path. There were none, which might mean it had been re-routed around the edges of fields or that the lie of the land prevented it being obvious. He planned to find out.

If he were still living at the vicarage, that would have been no problem. He would have slipped out of his room and gone for a walk as he had done any number of evenings. Ever since he had spoken the lie that he was coming and going from Harpury he had made walks virtually impossible.

He opened a can of tuna fish he had bought at the village shops and concocted a salad with lettuce from the cottage garden and an apple and carrots found in the kitchen. It did not feel like theft because the stuff would shrivel and be wasted if he did not eat it. Jenny had sadly told him about Mrs Pendle's death and her lack of relations close by. Jenny, in other words, had given him the idea of using the cottage.

He loved its serenity and did not want to upset it. Hardly anything had been disturbed since he had teased open the kitchen window on Wednesday evening to gain access. The house was as he had imagined it, except that there was no scent or sign of Mrs Pendle having kept a dog. The rattling of the letter box on Sunday became a mystery.

Most of his time there he lay on the bed and watched shadows shifting across fields and brightly coloured specks of cars through the hedgerow bordering the Harpury road. Only two things drew him downstairs: the kitchen and the television set.

While he was in the cottage he followed rules and one was not to use the television after dark when its glow could give his presence away. He switched on the set for the news, its sound deliberately low so nobody who came to the front door could hear it. A little into the programme there was an item which especially interested him.

It was peculiar seeing Benfield on television, particularly the shot of St John's. The reporter called it the 'Village of Fear' and behind him was the green without a soul in sight as though the inhabitants were too scared to venture out. Miles scoffed. Benfield was always like that during the afternoon. He could have told them.

The reporter said it was only two miles from where Mary Cross had been killed and then there was a bit of film which had been screened many times before, showing police at the field gateway on the morning she was found. After that the camera tracked up the Harpury road to Ayot crossroads and then the screen was filled with the shy face of Susan Dawlish.

'Susan was attacked close to where I'm standing,' said the reporter. 'She was walking through Ayot wood when a man battered her and left her for dead. But Susan staggered to an isolated cottage for help.'

Up came Meadow Cottage, which Miles could not recognize, and a repeated piece of film of the Jarmans. 'Susan', said the reporter, 'was unconscious by the time she was taken by ambulance to St Albans hospital. She is now in a neurosurgical unit fighting for her life.'

More rural shots and then slanting, jettied Church Cottages. 'Now Benfield has a third cause for fear,' said the reporter. 'Veronica Long, a pretty seventeen-year-old, has gone missing.' A full-length photograph of Veronica appeared and the camera moved in until she was cut off from the people pictured with her and the screen showed only her young face, smiling with the spurious innocence that Miles had hated when she challenged him with sleeping in the church.

After the reporter had set the scene there were interviews with a senior police officer who repeated an appeal for information about a man with brown hair and beard who was wanted in connection with the murder case. Then he renewed the pleas for help from anyone who had seen Susan Dawlish on Sunday evening. Finally he said gravely that concern for Veronica Long was mounting and it could not be ruled out that she might have become a third victim. There were reasons, he said, to believe that Mary Cross and Susan Dawlish could have been attacked by the same person.

Then it was back to the reporter at Benfield with some footage of the blackened part of the wood and the story of firemen and local people struggling to save cottages around the green. Yet another reason, he said, to dub Benfield the 'Village of Fear'.

Miles sat through the entire programme fascinated. He had never seen anywhere he knew well on television and wished Mrs Pendle had owned a video recorder so he could have played it over again. In his opinion the camera crew had cheated, filming in one place when they ought for the sake of accuracy to have been in another. And what were the police officer's reasons for believing Mary Cross's killer to be the same as Susan Dawlish's attacker? And why had concern for Veronica Long 'mounted' when the local gossip was that she had run away from home as she had done twice before?

Frustratingly there was no one to ask and he knew better than to talk to anyone in Benfield. They would guess rather than confess they understood no more than he did. When he had arrived in the village they had brought him their guesses about what lay beneath the plaster on the carvings. The only person he had directly asked was Stan Albury. The old chap had professed ignorance yet if anyone in the village had ever heard a story about the carvings, then Albury had.

He looked again at the map, carrying it to the window for better light. The wood where he had camped was clearly marked as Benfield Wood, the small copse near the crossroads was named Ayot Wood, and a house in the lane from the crossroads to Back Lane might be Meadow Cottage. He had noticed no name on it when walking that way.

A small anxiety fell away from him. Ayot wood and Benfield wood were two separate places and the police would not be tramping through Benfield wood and stumbling on what remained of his camp. He hung the map back up and went upstairs. The house he believed was possibly Meadow Cottage was visible, a red small-tiled roof with the sagging look of antiquity and white-painted walls. Miles decided to check on house and footpath in one dangerous outing.

From a wall cupboard he lifted out a man's dark green anorak with a hood. He was very pleased about the hood. The garment was too large for him and much too hot for the weather but it did what he wanted: it disguised his shape and made him anonymous. Shoes and trousers did not matter. He would put on the anorak and go in search of the footpath as soon as it was dusk.

Miles switched on the immersion heater for a bath when he returned. For a while he listened to the radio but the battery was running down and he needed to be sparing with it. Voices came from the lane once as boys cycled home to cottages on the green. Otherwise the silence was complete.

Judging it dark enough he set out. A couple of hundred yards down the lane, practically opposite a stile into Benfield wood, he found it. There was no sign declaring it a footpath but the opening in the hedge was obvious enough and when he was through he could see the shadow where the path lay, a slight dip in the surface of the field. Head down and affecting a limp to disguise his identity yet more, he hurried forward.

The field was empty but it was the first of three and in the other two were animals. Miles reached a gate. Beyond it there was no indication of a path, the dip having petered out a quarter of the way through the first pasture. He knew the map marked its continuation but could not see a gate on the far side of the second field and somewhere in the growing darkness were cattle. Miles kept to the rim of the field taking care not to miss a way out.

A number of times he winked his torch briefly to avoid falling in a ditch. And he was hot in the anorak, very hot. His slowness exasperated him and when he noticed a spot where the hedge was thin he forced a way through and began to cross the third field, keeping to the side. A pony, rising up in panic, sent him reeling and he had to switch on the torch and run while the animal's shrill terror roused its companions.

Miles abandoned his attempt to find where the path met the main road and fled, impeded by the bulky garment. Animals were rushing about, making the sort of commotion that could bring someone to see what had upset them. So far the expedition had been a disaster but he might yet find out the name of the house.

He battled through a weak point in a hedge and tumbled down on the far side, landing in a heap in a dry ditch. Torchlight picked out a white gatepost a hundred yards away. He snapped off the light and approached.

The house had a gable end wall abutting the lane and a gravelled courtyard beside it. At right angles to the house was a garage, its doors open showing it was empty. No lights were on. Miles glided forward, searching for a name on the barred gate to the courtyard. The gate was wide open and he entered, giving his attention to the front of the house. His torch lit neither a name on the door nor a plaque on the wall.

Just as he was admitting failure, a car turned into the lane at the crossroads. Miles was gripped with the fear of discovery. He would be suspected of attempted burglary at the very least. The police would come. There would be questions. He would hate it. He always hated questions.

It was too much to hope that the car was heading anywhere else. Few people used the lane because Benfield was served by better ones. He backed into the shadowed corner made by house and garage, knowing he did not have time to race across the courtyard. The car was already slowing. It began its turn, swinging wide to the far side of the lane so it could make a straight run into the garage.

Miles was in a state of trembling apprehension. Any second those headlights would hold him in their glare. He was torturing himself to think of an excuse to offer for being on private property but it was too late in the evening for conventional excuses and he could think of nothing. The headlights were straightening, a bright band of light sweeping in his direction. And then something gave way behind him. As he caught his balance he noticed he was leaning against a high wooden gate. Urgent hands sought a latch and he let himself into a garden.

The garden was black. Car lights went out and people were talking on the gravel, perhaps about to come through the gate to the back door. Miles dived into the blackness. On his right was the wall of the garage but, as he could not tell whether there was anywhere to hide beyond it, he went towards the house. He hurled himself round the corner, noting the position of the back door and aiming for cover among shrubs.

Miles collapsed on his knees behind a viburnum when someone switched on outside lights. He clamped a hand over his mouth as if that might quieten his ragged breathing. The side gate opened, voices started up and feet went as far the the back door. A woman remarked on the lingering scent of roses. Miles felt dizzy and sick, praying she would not walk over to sniff at them. He drew his hood up and held his face down. Despite a powerful urge to keep an eye on the couple, he feared them noticing the paleness of his face where there ought only to be shadows.

Then the back door was opened and in they went. Miles bit on the side of his fist. He silently begged them to put off their outside lights, lock their door and go to bed, let him get away. Instead, they let their dog out.

She was a moth-eaten, lethargic old bitch who had not stirred herself to complain about Miles's arrival. But once she was sent outside she rallied with a bark or two and trotted up to inspect him. Joining him behind the viburnum, she murmured in a puzzled fashion, went to relieve herself by the hedge and returned to him with a half-hearted growl.

Miles stretched out a hand to pat her but that was an unfortunate response because the growl was replaced by a series of barks. A man appeared in the doorway and shouted: 'Pansy, don't be silly. Come!' He called to his wife that Pansy was terrorizing another fieldmouse. Pansy obeyed and trotted indoors. Miles rubbed sweat from his face with the sleeve of the anorak. He was reprieved but he had yet to escape and his strength had deserted him.

For the first time he saw the couple, in their lighted kitchen window, and knew they were definitely the Jarmans. He recognized them from television. Therefore the house was equally definitely Meadow Cottage and a mystery was explained. It stood in the lane between Benfield wood and Ayot wood and the Jarmans believed Susan Dawlish had come to them from Ayot wood instead of from Benfield wood, which was nearer. The girl herself, new to the district, had apparently given the wrong name and nobody had challenged the information. If she were to die the mistake would never be corrected.

In the kitchen Mrs Jarman made a hot drink and Mr Jarman pottered about before the garden and kitchen were in darkness and lights appeared upstairs. Miles seized the moment and ran to the lee of the house, where, if they looked out, the Jarmans would not see him. He did not worry about Pansy because her warnings had already been rejected.

But his relief at reaching the garden gate was shortlived. The Jarmans had padlocked it. He had no hope of getting through. Intent on keeping intruders out, they had locked him in.

Miles retreated to the shadow of the house. A drain near him gurgled. A light went out behind the frosted glass of a first-floor bathroom. Soon, he thought, very soon the Jarmans would put out their bedroom light and he would be in utter darkness again. A curtain swung across a window and robbed him of most of his light.

Gingerly he felt to the top of the wooden gate. Wire. Sharp wire to deter anyone from climbing over. He was deterred. He edged his way along the side of the garage and behind it. There was a greenhouse against a wall and stacks of earthenware flower pots which he toppled. Indoors Pansy barked. Miles investigated the hedge that made the rest of the Jarmans' boundary but at each place he tried he found concealed in its depths a perfectly sound wire fence which made penetration impossible.

The last of the house lights went out committing him to disorientating darkness. Miles made a decision. On the back wall of the garage was a trellis supporting a clematis. The points where the trellis was secured to the wall might be strong enough to give him the foothold he needed to hoist himself on to the garage roof.

He felt the trellis break under his weight but it did not matter. He was up and scrambling across the roof, jumping over wire along the front of the roof and dropping down to invisible ground.

Miles was astounded by the amount of noise he made. He slid on landing, skinning his hands, and the hood fell back. Before he had found his feet Pansy was barking with more determination than he had given her credit for. Lights went on and a window was flung open. Miles threw himself at the barred gate which was now bolted across the courtyard entrance. He wasted no time with the bolts but rolled over it and hared away.

Covering the lane with a speed which surprised him he reached a field gate and cleared it. He lay panting where he fell until he was able to slow his breathing enough to listen hard. No one was after him. When he was fit to move he noticed the lights at Meadow Cottage, turned his back on them and set off along the edge of the field.

It was not one he had crossed earlier but was the best to be in as the crop was tall enough to give cover if needed. There were no alarms and he reached the cottage safely. Straight upstairs he hung the anorak in its cupboard, ran a bath, and found ointment for his stinging hand before rolling out the sleeping bag.

He decided that in the morning he should take his belongings to St John's. It was purely a precaution because he had not been told that Mrs Pendle was to be buried next day but the moment was drawing nearer when her relatives would look over the cottage. If the funeral was fixed for Friday they might stay there for the weekend. And he knew the funeral was imminent because Stan Albury had dug a grave.

21

The Reverend Adam King was anticipating a bad day. He disliked funerals and especially when the bereaved were travelling long distances and likely to be late. In his experience people never allowed sufficient time for journeys, particularly those on Fridays when road traffic was routinely heaviest. It was just his bad luck to have a funeral on a Friday.

He jabbed a spoon into the runny yolk of his breakfast egg and thought critical thoughts about Jenny who had failed to cook the egg the way he liked it. After six years of marriage she ought to know he liked eggs boiled until the yellow was crumbly.

Jenny was making a quick visit to an elderly man at Ayot St Martin for whom she had offered to shop while his daughter-in-law and son were on holiday. King's lips pursed with displeasure as he thought how her 'quick visit' would expand. She would feel obliged to do a little cleaning while she was there or organize some other woman to do it. Then she would be fussing over bedroom curtains with the 'wonderful' woman she had found to do the vicarage sewing. King could not say whether the woman's work was wonderful or not because the new sitting-room curtains had still not been hung. He supposed his wife was waiting for him to help her do that.

The back door opened and Jeffrey Miles came in enquiring about a cup of tea. And that was another thing, the Reverend Adam King complained in his head while his face did the smiling. Jeffrey Miles was another thing. He was there and not there, less approachable than he had been all those weeks

ago when he got off the bus by the village green and introduced himself. Lately it was hard to get a word out of him,
even about the carvings. Miles was, well, *possessive* about them
although goodness knows they were nothing to do with him.
And he would be rigidly cross when he was told to break off
that day, go and amuse himself while a service took place.

The vicar wanted his egg in peace. He wanted Jenny there to
pour the tea and he did not want Miles there looking dour and
making him uneasy. One day he must confront Miles with the
truth about the serpent of St John and he did not relish it. It
would be as difficult as arguing with Jenny: he would retreat
into pomposity and never know whether he had been taken
seriously. Miles, he suspected, would let him have his say but
not reveal what was in Miles's own mind. King doubted he
would ever find out whether Miles had realized the thing was
a basilisk.

He wondered whether to raise the subject that morning
when he went over to tell Miles about the funeral. Better not,
he decided, because Miles's reaction was unpredictable. If he
took it into his head to abandon the work the carvings might
never be finished. Progress had already slowed to a question-
able degree as though Miles were deliberately stretching out
the work. Mention of the basilisk must be delayed until it was
finished.

The vicar made himself toast, once Miles had gone, and
considered what he ought to say to Mrs Long when he made a
duty call that morning. 'Don't worry' would no longer do
when the police were making statements about 'mounting
concern'. His own concern had existed from the start and as
each hour passed without word from the girl it deepened.
People had reported sightings of her from all over the country
yet none had proved genuine. It was confusing that young
girls chose to look alike with identical clothes and hairstyles.

But hanging most heavily on King's mind was Sunday's
sermon. Quite honestly he knew he was not one of the great
sermon makers and, although he could get by on a week-to-
week basis, whenever something peculiar happened in the
parish he found it difficult to judge whether he should make it
the springboard for a sermon.

143

The first year Jenny brought the morris men to the village green for maypole dancing he thought it a neat idea to refer to the event because it was of considerable local interest and even a little controversial. But afterwards, as the meagre congregation trooped out of St John's, one of the regular attenders made a remark about never expecting to hear paganism preached from the pulpit. Jenny roared with laughter when he relayed it but he was never fully convinced it was a joke.

And now he had a murder, an attack on one young woman and the disappearance of a third, not to mention the destruction of Benfield wood. 'Oh dear,' he sighed as he finished the toast and wiped buttery fingers on his napkin. Sermons were simply not his thing.

Jenny sped back from Ayot St Martin and went directly to see Mrs Long. The woman had got her other daughters off to school and arrived at the time of morning when there was nothing to occupy her but Veronica's absence. Jenny saw from her face there had been no telephone call.

The woman looked drawn, her hair more unkempt than usual. 'When she went the other times,' she explained, repeating herself, 'there were phone calls. She was only nine the first time. She caught the bus outside the vicarage to go to Hertfield to look for her friend who'd moved away from the village. She rang to say so as soon as she got off at the bus station and I called the police. They brought her home.'

Jenny managed a kindly interest although she found the adventure irrelevant because nine-year-olds and seventeen-year-olds have markedly different motives for running off. Mrs Long went on to the second stage of the story: 'And when she was fourteen Veronica hitched a lift in a car to London and took a train to Brighton. She had enough pocket money by that age to save up the fare, you see. Well, she left it twenty-four hours before ringing me and she wouldn't say where she was. Three weeks she was away that time. Just came back saying she'd been for a holiday and met some people on the beach and stayed at their place. She came back when her money ran out. She couldn't get a job because she looked young for her age and wouldn't have fooled anyone into taking her on.'

There was more of it but none had much bearing on Veronica's current disappearance. 'How much money did she take this time?' Jenny brought Mrs Long back to the present.

'I don't know that she took much. Her savings book is in her bedroom and she hasn't drawn out a lot, not since Christmas when it got very low because of presents.'

Mrs Long said the police had asked her about her daughter's savings and also about clothes. 'She went on the spur of the moment,' she told Jenny. 'Just upped and went as she was, no luggage or anything.' She forced a weak smile. 'When she was nine she took my shopping bag with all sorts of stuff: her best nightie, a change of underwear and some biscuits in case she felt hungry.'

While the woman talked on Jenny asked herself how long her loyalty to Veronica could have lasted if she had been using Pendle Cottage. She did not see how she could have protected Veronica's independence instead of rushing to tell her mother she was safe. The whole village would have got to hear of it, Veronica would have been humiliated and not forgiven her and, quite possibly, Veronica would have run away to London.

On her way home from Mrs Long's cottage Jenny saw Miles in the churchyard. Unusually, he was sitting in the sun looking relaxed. On impulse she went to him hoping it was an opportunity for a conversation. 'Lovely day, Jeff,' she called, wearing her most winning smile.

Miles's spirits slumped. What could she want at the church? She was either coming to pester him, to try to involve him in one of her dreadful village activities, or else she was going to demand to see the carvings. Well, hard luck. He was not going to get involved and he would not have her up on his platform even if she had been miraculously cured of her fear of ladders.

Jenny watched the wariness seep back into his face. Just a light dying in the eyes, just a tightening of the jaw. All the difference. She ignored the difference. She was not going to be chased away by him. But she meant to be careful and not, for instance, ask about the carvings or say anything else to which he might, quite unreasonably, object.

She leaned a hand on the warm stone porch and surveyed

Benfield as he had been doing. Eighteenth-century vicarage, a wood, green slopes, and trees around tombstones honey-coloured in the sun. She spoke only about the weather, the length of the dry spell and the grumbles of the farmers. But she was tossing up whether this was a good time to announce she knew he had moved into her friend's cottage and hoped to arrange for him to stay.

Before she made a decision Miles said: 'You must miss Mrs Pendle.'

Jenny was touched by this sympathy. In anyone else it would have been unremarkable but Jeffrey Miles was one of the coldest people she had known. Shyness was an awful impediment to a full life, she thought. She said: 'It's very upsetting to lose a friend as quickly as that but it was better for her.' She shunned the memory of her friend dead in the passage, clawing at the front door in an agonized attempt to get help. Sympathetic remarks required only conventional responses.

Miles said: 'They've picked a good spot for her.'

For a second Jenny did not understand. Then she looked where he was looking, up the graveyard towards the western gate. The open grave was not visible from where they were but both knew it was wide and waiting. Jenny said: 'Oh no, that's not for Mrs Pendle. Old Mr Dingley died at the geriatric hospital and they're bringing him here for burial this afternoon. I shouldn't think you ever heard of him, Jeff. He went into hospital a couple of years ago and never came home.'

The back door of the vicarage was opening. Jenny got as far as: 'Mrs Pendle won't be buried . . .' when her husband called that she was wanted on the telephone. With rapid apologies to Miles, Jenny hurried away. He finished her sentence in his mind: 'Mrs Pendle won't be buried, she'll be cremated.'

He was relieved the funeral was not Mrs Pendle's, that the family would not turn him out of the cottage for the weekend. But he was disgusted with the vicar. When he had gone to the vicarage, pretending to want a drink but actually giving the man an opportunity to tell him when a funeral was to be held, King had scarcely spoken to him.

Miles shunned the sun and went into St John's. He began to

work with febrile haste as if to make up for the time to be lost during the Dingley funeral. The vicar had not discussed the carvings with him for days but the conversation he had overheard, between Jenny and her friend Don, had left him in no doubt that King studied them secretly at night. He jabbed away at the plaster.

His attitude to the carvings had changed because the spirit of their creator no longer entered him. As the saintly figures of the first panels had come to life in his hands he had been thrilled by their beauty. And then he had come upon the basilisk and it had altered him. No saint enchanted him as that did. He marvelled at the bravura of the craftsman who dared dedicate his finest work to a symbol of evil in the company of saints. But that peak of exhilaration, when Miles's fingertips on the scales of the beast released the creator's spirit, was past.

The St Francis had been a let down. Miles grudged time spent on the delicate business of cleaning it perfectly. Having identified the subject he had been impatient to move on to the next panel, hoping for another fabulous creature who would revive in him what had been lost. When he had found a St Stephen he left the panel roughly cleaned and skipped to the next. A few details of this had been opened up, enough for the symbols to convey St Michael. Miles had abandoned him too and rushed on, desperate for a discovery which would let him relive the secret joy of the days when the basilisk illuminated his life.

The vicar told him the time of the Dingley funeral and Miles said he would go for a walk while it took place. He cleaned up as much as he could and then a woman standing in for Mrs Long arrived to dust.

Miles went to Ayot crossroads, passing Meadow Cottage and seeing no sign of a name board. At the crossroads he turned south on to the Harpury road and strolled along on the grass verge, ostensibly watching horses in the fields but actually seeking a footpath. There was neither a path nor a good point to get through the hedge. Although it was low it was backed by wire.

Half a mile south he turned east into another lane which led to Benfield and at the shop bought enough food for the weekend. He completed the square by walking up the road to the church, sparing a glance at Mrs Long's open door. Reedy singing came from St John's. The service had begun late. Miles did not know what to do. He had his shopping but nowhere to put it until he could stow the things in his bag on the platform. If he took the shopping to the vicarage Jenny's curiosity would be aroused about his fictitious arrangements in Harpury. If he stood outside the church with it the mourners would find it distinctly out of place.

He walked to the wood, stepped a little way into the trees and set the plastic bag down against an oak. The singing ended. The church door opened and figures appeared in the porch.

There were about a dozen mourners, several Miles recognized as village folk. They moved in a bunch from the porch to the graveside, keeping pace with the slowest. The oldest were supported on the arms of younger friends and a couple of women at the tail end exchanged a discreet joke. A breeze lifted the Reverend Adam King's brown hair from his crown as he said the words and a woman anchored her hat with her hand.

The breeze carried the sounds across to the wood: the vicar's clear voice, the shuffle of feet, the sobbing of a granddaughter and the furtive rustling of paper handkerchiefs as mourners dabbed eyes. Above it all a lark sang.

After the dejected party trailed away Miles emerged with his shopping and went to the platform. He did some desultory work but his heart was not in it. He had problems. His escape route would not work and he did not know whether the Pendle service was to held in St John's. Even if there was to be no burial or memorial service at St John's, Jenny would certainly go to the cremation. By asking her about that he could find out how soon he might be disturbed at the cottage.

He went to the vicarage to try and see her but was unlucky. He found nobody about except Stan Albury, his back bent to his sombre task. The sound of earth filling the space above old Mr Dingley's coffin rang as Miles took the footpath to Pendle Cottage.

22

The vicarage was not empty when Jeffrey Miles called but seeing him coming out of the churchyard the vicar decided to ignore him in favour of a page of scribbled notes which would, by dint of weekly miracle, turn into a sermon before he went to bed. Saturdays were no use. There was always far too much interruption for clear thought. And Sunday mornings were too late. He felt justified in ignoring Miles and giving priority to his scribbles.

His day was going as badly as he had feared. The Dingley daughter had been late, having got lost near Watford, and he'd had to delay. A vague cousin or out-of-touch friend could have been discounted but he was not heartless enough to start a funeral without a daughter. And then Stan Albury had shuffled into the back of the church wearing his working clothes, which is to say sagging cord trousers and a torn plaid shirt that looked like a lumberjack's cast-off.

King had not realized Albury and Dingley had ever been friends. Certainly Dingley's stories about Benfield life never gave that impression yet there must have been something between them for Albury to choose to pay his respects. And the old chap had shown enough sense of decency to hang back in the church when they went to the graveside rather than appear among the mourners dressed like that.

King thought it too bad of Jeffrey Miles to lurk in the wood spying. What on earth had he thought he was doing? Anybody could have seen him if that white plastic bag had caught an eye. Sheer luck no one had glanced that way. As it was, Miles's staring had put King off and he made a slip with the words. No matter. The mourners probably did not notice and the loved one was buried more or less according to the rites of the Church of England even if the clergy had been a doubtful benefit.

The vicar heard the sound of his back door and Miles scrunching over the yard towards the church. Shortly after, he saw him carrying his bag towards the far gate. He slammed down his pen and went to fetch himself tea. The kettle was cold. Miles had not bothered as no one was there to make it for him. The vicar reached for the tea caddy.

Jenny was in Hertfield shopping. She had been scampering about all day and he had been the one to answer the telephone and the door although they were supposed to have an agreement that she protected him from them on Fridays because that was sermon day. He spooned tea into the pot.

He was still toying with a sermon which linked the burning of the wood with the death of Mary Cross, the attack on Susan Dawlish and anxiety about Veronica. But he could not see his way through to a conclusion. A hellfire preacher, he thought, would have no trouble in saying such sufferings were the wages of sin. He fetched a tea strainer and thought, with irony and no smile, that he should tie Benfield's tragedies to the uncovering of the evil eye in St John's – and watch the entire congregation leave the church at a gallop!

Thinking of the basilisk sent him on his way to see the carvings before shadows deepened. Stan Albury was tidying up near the new grave and gave the comic salute he used in greeting. Inside the church King was folded in the calm which had so impressed him the first time he walked in. He had been remarkably fortunate to be offered St John's, a pretty church in an unspoiled village. The whole parish was a delight. Jenny had expected him to want a city parish, or at least one in a town, and talked in terms of challenge. But he'd had enough of that when he was a curate. He had not known its name then but what he had craved was Benfield.

A frown marred his high forehead. The basilisk. Every time he came through the door his eyes lifted to meet the basilisk's. They always would. If he had kept quiet about the panel the matter would be no more than a personal irritation but he had gushed about his wonderful serpent of St John the

Evangelist and made it inevitable that one colleague or another would drop into the church to admire it and recognize it for what it was.

He might even have to seek high-level advice about leaving it exposed or covering it up again. The very thought sent a flush of embarrassment through him. He would be known throughout the diocese as that fool who did not know a serpent from a basilisk. The bishop, magnanimously, would excuse his ignorance but the episode could tell against him when his name was discussed for future appointments. At that moment the Reverend Adam King wished he had never dreamed of opening the panels, never asked Jenny's cousin to find him Jeffrey Miles.

He climbed the ladder. From below it was unclear what the most recently exposed panels represented. He moved along the row, spending some time studying the detail. St Francis was splendid but . . . Why had Miles not finished in the bottom right-hand corner? Residue of plaster clung there. The vicar took a pen from his pocket and gouged gently. Plaster came away freely. Puzzled, King moved to the next panel. More residue, quite a lot more. He came to one where only part of a scene, enough to establish the stoning of St Stephen, had been cleared before the panel was abandoned in favour of the next. But once the winged and armoured figure of St Michael had become apparent Miles had given that up too.

For several minutes more the vicar crouched on Jeffrey Miles's platform looking at the evidence. His initial puzzlement turned to anger that Miles was skimping the job but then anger was replaced by concern for Miles. The young man had started well. He had cared deeply – too deeply, perhaps – about the stones but a drastic change had come over him. He had grown slapdash and feverishly impatient. Carvings as well as the standard of his own work had suffered. The vicar rubbed fingertips over scratches inflicted by Miles's uncaring haste. St Michael's wing was actually chipped!

Miles will have to be stopped, King decided. And it was a daunting decision because Miles was not an easy person and a complaint would be immensely difficult to handle. The vicar got to his feet, brushed plaster from his trouser legs, and went down the ladder. Miles was no longer respecting the carvings and would have to be stopped, whatever unpleasantness that caused.

The easiest thing, King thought, was to get Jenny's help. He would show her the damage, bully her into getting up the ladder to see for herself so she could not say he was exaggerating. Then he would ask her to tackle Miles, tell him to stop the work and find out what was wrong with him. She could handle it if anyone could, she was so good with people, although it was, strictly speaking, his responsibility. King put that responsibility out of his head. He had a sermon to finish and there was the whole weekend to decide what to do about Miles.

As he reached the lowest rung the church door opened. Stan Albury poked his head in, looking towards the altar as though that was the most probable place to find a vicar.

'I'm over here, Stan.' The last thing he wanted to hear was one of Stan's grouses but he supposed he would have to. It had been that sort of day.

'About the funeral, Vicar,' Albury began.

King winced. Surely not a ticking off for stumbling over the words? Was it possible one of the mourners had complained to Albury? King said with a slight challenge in his voice: 'Everything went off all right.'

'Oh, not old Dingley. I mean Mrs Pendle.'

'It's all in hand. What's bothering you, Stan?'

'Well, it's not for me to say, Vicar, but as I'm here and you're here it might be a good opportunity, as you might say, for us to take a look. Make sure everything *is* all right.'

Relieved that Albury was troubled by nothing more than conscientiousness, the vicar agreed. Better get it over with, he thought and led the way to the vestry. When he opened the desk drawer, Albury stabbed a hand forward and said: 'That's the key, Vicar.'

They went together to open the door to the Dornaye vault and see that there would be no difficulties on Monday when the mortal remains of Ada Pendle, née Dornaye, joined her ancestors. And that was how they found the body of Veronica Long.

23

Jenny was in pursuit of R. Dales, editor of *Angles*. The Hertfield office was closed and the greengrocer told her he had an idea the editor lived in Harpury and worked most of the time from home.

The undulating road carried her away beyond the boundaries of the parish she knew intimately and towards villages she had never visited. Campion brightened the hedgerows, wheatfields ripened to gold, there were excitable bluetits and tail-swishing horses in the shade of beeches. Jenny's mind was not on the tame beauty of the Hertfordshire countryside: she was thinking what to say to R. Dales when she caught him. It ought not to take long to establish whether the Dales of *Angles* and the Dale who lived at Common Close were the same person.

Harpury was bigger than she remembered. Buildings looked pieced together from scraps of different styles: shop fronts were late twentieth-century, above them were Georgian windows and above those were twisted tiled roofs centuries older. She crawled by the shops, slowed by Friday-afternoon traffic. Common Close suggested a location further on, in what people who were tricked by the modern frontages of the shopping centre sometimes called Old Harpury. When the buildings gave way to grass she stopped and asked a couple of old men on a bench for Common Close. They said fork right. Sun blinded her as she entered the close, eight anaemic houses.

The picture window of number five threw back a reflection of trees and brilliant sky but once Jenny was near the front door she could see into the empty dining room. While an electronic 'Greensleeves' responded to her pressing the bell she heard running steps and a woman on the other side of the door called: 'Who is it?'

Jenny gave her name and that was enough for the sound of bolts and chains to begin. She switched on a smile, ready to reassure.

Sheila Dale had been reassured as soon as she heard a female voice. Whoever had come, it could not be the Demon of Benfield. The morning papers were now calling him that although, naturally, the people of Harpury were adamant that he was no longer near Benfield.

Sheila and Jenny looked at each other. Jenny saw a thin wasted woman with faded skin and hair and the haunted face of the chronically anxious. She was immediately sure she had come to the wrong house, that Dale and Dales were independent and she must extricate herself swiftly. First she had to say something.

'I'm Jenny King,' she repeated. 'I'm looking for a Mr Dales.'

'Roger? What do you want him for?' Sheila did not quibble about that extraneous final 's', people had made that mistake with the name before.

Jenny covered her surprise at being at the right house after all and suggested they talk inside. In the sitting room she began cautiously, prepared for the woman to be an unsuspecting wife who had never heard of *Angles*. She said: 'I believe your husband edits a magazine, Mrs Dales?'

'That's right,' said Sheila thinking of *Pinboard*.

Totally sure she had the right house, the right wife and the right man. Jenny plunged on and said she wanted to meet Mr Dales and talk about the magazine.

'But he's in his office,' Sheila said. 'I'm sorry, I don't understand why you thought he'd be here.' She was wringing her hands, one of her wrists protected by a bandage.

Jenny said something vague about being told he worked from home. Sheila had invited her to sit down but had not done so herself and they were facing each other in the middle of the room. Sheila looked the length of it and fiddled with her bandage, saying: 'They make him work terrible hours and then there's the travelling to and from the office. I . . .' She collected herself and gave a tremulous smile. 'You didn't go to his office, did you?'

'Yes, but there was no one there.' Jenny also looked down the room and saw the broken french window, the makeshift repair with plastic sheeting. She was making the connection between the broken glass and the bandaged wrist when Sheila spoke again.

'He might be home in an hour. I suppose you could wait if it's important.' It seemed it must be exceptionally important for Jenny King to have gone to Brigges's office in London and then all the way to Harpury. She hoped it did not mean trouble.

Jenny decided to get as much information as she could out of the wife and catch the husband another time. However, Sheila became obtuse.

'I've seen the magazine,' Jenny said patiently. 'I know exactly what it's like so you don't have to pretend.' She waited but the glazed look did not leave Sheila's face. An explanation offered itself to Jenny and she asked: 'Haven't you ever seen a copy of it?'

A nod. 'I'm sorry, but what you say doesn't make sense. How can there be anything offensive about Roger's magazine?'

'I'd have thought that was obvious to any woman. And it's fallen into the hands of at least one village girl.'

Sheila thrust fingers through her once-pretty hair. 'I'm sorry . . . I *don't* see anything objectionable. How could there be?'

Jenny took a deep breath and began again, slowly and explicitly. The magazine showed titillating pictures of young females, its advertisements were the type notorious for luring girls into pornography, and so on.

Suddenly Sheila gave a hysterical laugh. 'You're crazy! Roger's magazine isn't like that. I don't know where you got the idea but it's the wrong one.'

'Mrs Dales, I've seen it. He came to Benfield to apologize to me after I'd complained . . .'

Sheila clutched her hair with both hands. 'No!' she shrieked. 'No, you're making this up. I don't understand why but you are. It's a very dull magazine. Really it is. It's all pictures of factories and circuit boards.'

Jenny gaped. The woman was not putting on a defensive act. Her reaction was genuine, her emotion dangerously raw. Sheila gabbled on, a long rejection of the nonsensical accusation she had just heard. When at last she broke off, having overexcited herself to the stage where she was incoherent and shaking, there came in the lull the sound of a car pulling on to the drive.

Both women turned their heads towards the sound. Jenny was choosing how to proceed. Believe Sheila and apologize to her husband for upsetting his vulnerable wife because of a mistake of identity? Or stand by her belief that she had come to the right house? There were too many coincidences if the editor of *Angles* were not the man living at 5 Common Close.

Roger Dale came into the sitting room. As he took in the scene – Jenny poised for flight and Sheila with the back of her hand to her mouth – he knew something had gone badly wrong. Sheila gave him time to cope because she rushed in with the story that Jenny had made silly accusations about his magazine. 'She says it's pornographic and insulting and . . .'

Years ago Dale had created a loophole and now he prepared to slip through it. First he asked Sheila what she had replied. Her answer reassured him she had not found out about *Angles*. He switched his smile to the visitor, guessing who she was. 'I'd better put your mind at rest, Mrs er . . .'

'King. Jenny King.' She had decided to stick to her guns and added: 'You called at the vicarage last week to see me but I was out.'

Dale raised a quizzical eyebrow. 'What vicarage?' His loophole would help him escape from Jenny King.

'Benfield.' Jenny saw him deny all knowledge of her with a mystified shake of the head. Her confidence in her theory dwindled. She felt foolish and guilty at having troubled a woman who was plainly sick. The best thing to do was make her apology and get out.

Dale was heading for his loophole. He repeated: 'I'd better

set your mind at rest, hadn't I, Mrs King? Let me show you a copy of my magazine.'

She choked back the assertion that she had seen it and stood awkwardly while Dale fetched a briefcase from the hall and took out a copy of *Pinboard*. She did not want to take it but he held it steadily towards her.

When it was in her hand he said ironically: 'I'm prepared to offer a small prize to whichever of you finds any pornography in that.' He smiled at Sheila in a way which said she was not to upset herself any more, everything was fine except that her visitor was unhinged.

Jenny turned over the pages, hands clumsy in her embarrassment. Husband and wife were joined in unspoken condemnation. She put the magazine down. There was only one thread of hope that she had not made an utter fool of herself. She asked whether *Pinboard* was the only publication Dale edited. He snapped the thread and told her it was.

Bravely she apologized, saying she had been looking for the editor of *Angles*. Dale smiled a forgiving smile and stepped through his loophole. 'Our names are very alike but I refuse to be blamed for *Angles*.'

Jenny drove off subdued, horrified by her ridiculous mistake and its consequences. This feeling was to last most of the way home but suddenly she stopped thinking about her stupidity and considered Roger Dale more keenly.

He had proof that he edited *Pinboard*, Brigges's house magazine, but was there no chance that, despite his easy denial, he was also involved with *Angles*? Whoever edited it was seldom at the Hertfield office and the greengrocer thought he lived in Harpury. That two men with names so similar should be magazine editors was coincidence enough. For them both to live in a place as small as Harpury was piling coincidence suspiciously thick.

She was hatching a plot to lure the *Angles* editor to the Hertfield office when up the road near the vicarage she saw police cars. Jenny was forced to park in the road and go the rest of the way on foot. A knot of people stood by the church gate. Police vehicles blocked the vicarage drive. She ran, seized with dread.

'What's happened?' she demanded but the villagers knew nothing. She squeezed by the cars and went to the rear of the vicarage. No one was there. Low voices came from the churchyard. As she ran there men emerged from St John's with a burden.

A lump rose in her throat and she shuddered to a halt. They were carrying something covered. Some*one* covered. A dead body was being taken away. After the men came her husband, ashen. Jenny went to him. Emotion churned her words but she got out: 'Who, Adam?'

His unfocused eyes did not see her. They were still seeing the scream on the face of Veronica Long, the face he had illuminated when, to satisfy Stan Albury that there was space for Mrs Pendle's remains, he flashed a torch among the dusty coffins in the vault. Marks in the dust showed how the body had been dragged across the floor from the entrance. It was arranged on the flagstones in an attitude of death with hands folded across breasts and face looking up to heaven. When the police surgeon moved it he found the damage to the back of the skull and black clotted blood in the hair.

Jenny shook Adam's arm, rapping out questions until he told her what had been in the vault. The bright day dimmed. She was afraid she was going to faint. There was a nauseating heat about her face and her knees weakened. She staved it off. Adam did not linger but continued down the path to the vicarage. She staggered after him, shaping more questions and frightened of the answers. Above her a lark sang and the church clock struck.

Adam was in the kitchen when she caught up. He was not doing anything, just standing with a hand to his forehead and his eyes shut. Jenny understood. 'You're going with them, aren't you? To tell Mrs Long.'

There was a nearly imperceptible nod. She groaned. 'Oh, Adam . . .'

He turned his back on her and said in an ugly tone: 'Veronica didn't go to London, did she? She walked out of this house and got herself murdered.'

Jenny was appalled. 'You're blaming me! You're saying

it's my fault because I didn't pack her off home when she needed to talk.'

'You knew there'd been a murder. She shouldn't have been wandering about on her own.'

Jenny insisted that Veronica had been entitled to walk where she liked and her home was only three hundred yards from the entrance to the vicarage drive. Adam asked her how she would like to go and tell that to Mrs Long.

They were interrupted by a police officer. 'We're going down to the house now, Mr King.' The vicar followed him out.

Later, Jenny thought. Later she would have to go to the house too. She would have nothing helpful or encouraging to say but she would have to go and let her presence show the family she shared their distress. If she wanted to share in the fun of the village, she had to share in its tragedies too.

Yet she could not accept what had happened. Even Adam's harshness had not persuaded her Veronica was dead. The fact was too terrible to be absorbed. She thought bitterly how much worse it would be for the Longs.

A couple of local men came to the back door to ask her what she knew about events at the church. Down at the gate the police had refused to explain anything. 'They brought a body out. We know that much,' said one of the men, wheedling her to reveal the rest.

Jenny imagined the inquisitive congregating outside Church Cottages before the police had finished there. She wondered why the men had not dogged Adam and the police along the street instead of coming to her. Hedging, she said it was not for her to say, there had been nothing official and so forth.

The man coaxed: 'Come on, Jenny. We know you know all about it.'

But his companion nudged him and made him give it up. Jenny King was clearly upset.

When they had gone she latched the back door, poured a brandy and took it to one of the sitting-room windows. She was quaking as she sipped.

'Veronica's dead,' she said aloud in a voice as firm as she

could manage. 'I didn't send her home and so she's dead.' Even when the words were spoken the fact was not believable.

A while later, standing there with her empty glass in her hand, Jenny saw movement in the shrubbery and the police officers Adam had accompanied appeared on the lawn. She went out to meet them. 'Your husband's idea, Mrs King,' said one. 'He said Veronica used to take a short cut this way to her mother's back door and we ought to use it to avoid half the village trailing after us.'

Before she could comment the police were asking her for information. Boyfriends, they said. Did she know anything about a man Veronica used to meet? Her mother had heard rumours but no names and the police wanted to interview such a man if he existed. 'We're told she talked a lot to you, Mrs King. Was a man mentioned? What do you remember?'

But she could not help. 'There's something else you ought to know, though,' she said and told them what she had previously withheld when Veronica was merely a missing person. 'Veronica was trying to get work as a photographic model. She wrote offering to work for a man advertising in a magazine.' Jenny looked from one face to the other. Polite. No quickening of interest. She pushed on, wanting it over before Adam returned and heard how much she had to say.

To her own ears it sounded disappointingly tame but Veronica was dead and the girl's secrets would have to be exposed if her killer was to be caught. Then, in a torrent, before she gave herself time to judge the wisdom of it, Jenny said what had been running through her mind all the time she had been drinking her brandy and convincing herself of Veronica's death. The police interest sharpened. If what Jenny King was telling them proved true they could be close to arresting the Demon of Benfield.

24

By Saturday morning Pauline Williams had exhausted all possible excuses. Veronica Long was no longer a missing girl, she was a murder victim. Mary Cross had been dead two months. Susan Dawlish might yet die. Pauline relinquished the scruples which had prevented her ringing the police and pointing out that Roger Dale had a false alibi for the time Mary died, that he frequented the area where Susan was attacked and that he had received a letter from someone signing herself Veronica Long.

She did not rehearse, she got on the line and coolly explained to an attentive female voice. Until her words were out she did not entirely believe she had the temerity to invite them to consider Roger Dale a murderer.

Afterwards she had a sensation of anticlimax. Matters were out of her hands. Only then did she realize what an alarming amount of her time she had let the question of Dale's guilt occupy. She feared she had become obsessed with it.

Trying to put the whole business out of her mind she planned an outing to an exhibition, a browse in a bookshop with a good travel section, a film, a visit to her flatmate in hospital. It was one thing to ring the police but another to hang around the flat waiting self-importantly in case they called on her. She went out.

Curiosity about what was happening to Dale bobbed in and out of her head all day. By evening, guilt was causing her pain. What did her suspicions amount to after all? Not much, although the policewoman had not been unkind enough to suggest that. Pauline was convincing herself that Dale's wife and children would endure awful embarrassment before he was cleared because of an obvious fact which she, a spiteful secretary, had been too stupid to see. She felt ashamed, as though in doing a public duty she had failed in a personal loyalty.

Although she never knew it none of this mattered a jot because she was not the first to point the finger at Roger Dale. Jenny King had already done it. By the time Pauline dialled the police number, two officers were on Dale's doorstep listening to 'Greensleeves'. One was Sergeant Travis of the sandy hair and alert young face.

Dale was not altogether surprised to see him, not after Jenny King's visit to the house. He assumed it would be like her to go to the police when she failed to trace and berate the editor. And they would know where to find him. They already had.

Travis said good morning, they would like a word with him and could they come in? Dale took them into the dining room because the children were watching television in the sitting room. Sheila was next door with Mrs Catesby, helping her word a newspaper advertisement offering a reward for the return of her dog.

The police did not sit down which Dale hoped meant they would soon go. Travis said: 'The stuff we took away from the *Angles* office is under consideration, Mr Dale, but something else has come up.'

A voice in Dale's head explained: *'A complaint from a member of the public. No chance of dodging prosecution now.'*

The door opened and Caroline stared in with the unself-consciousness of an eight-year-old. She seemed about to ask her father a question when Sheila appeared behind her. A protective hand dropped on her daughter's shoulder and she drew the child back, although her own surprise at finding two policemen in her dining room was equal.

'Not that accident again?' Sheila said, addressing Dale.

'Yes. It's nothing to worry about.' He shut the door in her face. Then, to Travis: 'I told her you came the other evening about a traffic accident. She gets very worked up. There's no point in upsetting her.'

Travis said: 'I understand, Mr Dale. But you're going to

have to tell her something or other because we'd like you to come to Hertfield police station with us. It could take some time.'

Dale pictured himself cooped up in a room with copies of *Angles* spread on a desk and a narrow-minded police officer demanding the identity of the photographers (most of whom were Dale under pseudonyms), the names of models (most of which he could not remember) and the identity of box-number advertisers (who would then be scared off, cutting the magazine's income). Inevitably they would discover that he had filled out the shortfall in advertisements in some issues by inserting some himself: a box number in some cases and in others an advertisement carrying Brigges's address because Lomax had banned him from having replies directed to the office.

He saw no way of escaping prosecution. If the police were going to the trouble of taking him to Hertfield for a long session, then they were in deadly earnest. He had ducked through their road blocks with artwork and magazines in the boot of his car but they had got him all the same.

And Sheila. He would go on lying to her as long as he could but once the court case was imminent she would have to learn the truth. What would the truth do to Sheila? She was not strong enough to cope with it and it would be pathetic to watch her try. Even if a further lie tided him over the court hearing, subsequent publicity about the case would never escape her. Then she would run off to her parents, taking Timothy and Caroline away from him.

Dale shut out his fear for his children, it was too painful. He imagined other consequences of a pornography prose-cution. Al Lomax would drop him. No more glamour photo-graphy magazine. No more dog fighting. Lomax would demand his money back, money which had been spent on the darkroom and equipment. A comic consequence occurred to Dale and he could not help smiling. That sanctimonious old frump Pauline Williams would love every minute of his discomfort, especially as Brigges would have to sack him and she would get a new boss.

'Is something amusing you, Mr Dale?' asked Travis.

Dale's mind focused on his present predicament. 'No,' the voice in his head replied, 'nothing the police would find at all funny.' Aloud he said: 'Look, you turn your car round and I'll follow you.'

They had organized it like that last time but Travis refused. 'We're asking you to come in our car, Mr Dale.'

Dale objected. Travis said: 'Mr Dale, we aren't purely concerned with *Angles* today. I've told you that's under consideration . . .'

'What, then?' A terrible premonition clutched him. Despite the attack on Susan Dawlish they were still interested that he had been seen near the scene of Mary Cross's murder.

He was astonished when, instead of mentioning Mary Cross, Travis said: 'Veronica Long, Mr Dale. We believe you may be able to help us with our inquiries.'

In the back of the unmarked police car Dale thought what a silly phrase that was. 'Help' sounded like something freely given. A man who wanted to help their inquiries would have trotted off to the police station on his own initiative, he would not be dragged there by two policemen.

It was fortunate, he thought, that Common Close had only eight houses and few of the occupants were home on Saturday mornings. Only a handful of people had seen him slide into the back of the car beside Travis's colleague. Why, he wondered, had the colourless young man sat beside him? Did they expect their reluctant passenger to hurl himself from the moving car and run off?

Dale gave a sideways look but the man was gazing straight ahead. The car went over Ayot crossroads. It passed the spot where Mary Cross had lain. 'Don't look at the gateway,' the voice in Dale's brain screamed. 'Don't look!'

Hertfield police station was red-brick Victorian. Plenty of Saturday shoppers saw Dale driven into the car park behind it. Women with baskets on wheels and men with parcels in their arms peered at him. He hated them, hated their stupid, gawping faces and their assumption that anyone in the back of a police car was as good as found guilty.

Inside the police station he saw pinned on a wall a poster of the photofit picture. 'Have you seen this man?' the caption asked. Well, they had, hadn't they? They'd got him, hadn't they? He had no doubt the police and the people in the street were equally confident of it.

Dale anticipated the sort of long wait he had read about when people were left in dull rooms until their patience and their nerves gave and they were ready to offer their 'help'. It did not happen like that in Hertfield that day. A bulky but brisk inspector called Welford appeared quickly and came straight to the point. 'We have reason to believe you could have had contact with Veronica Long through your photography magazine, Mr Dale.'

Dale shook his head. 'What reason can you have to believe that?'

Welford was sitting across a table from him, square hands spread on its polished surface and sweat stains growing beneath his armpits. The room was hot although the window was open. Welford seemed resigned to the discomfort. He looked like a man who was not afraid to take his time.

He said: 'Veronica was hoping to become a model. She told someone she'd answered a magazine advertisement placed by someone wanting models.'

Dale thought this a bit thin. There was no shortage of magazines in the field, she could have answered advertisements in any of them. He said, quite truthfully, that he did not remember ever hearing of her. 'Mine isn't the likeliest magazine for her to have used. It's not on bookstalls, it's only available on subscription.'

'Quite,' said Welford in a tone which condemned the magazine while accepting Dale's point. 'But we know a copy came into her possession.'

The two men looked at each other closely. Dale considered the link with the girl tenuous but wondered about the name of the youngster who had written to him a couple of weeks earlier. At the time he had been more concerned with getting the new issue out and afterwards with the Sandra Sutton débâcle. He could not even remember what had become of the letter.

Welford said: 'Veronica lived at Benfield, Mr Dale, and . . .'

Dale cut in. 'I'm certain I've never had a letter from anyone at Benfield.'

Welford continued: 'You went to Benfield on Friday evening last week. You said so at a checkpoint. Were you going to see Veronica?'

Dale denied it flatly, avoiding any emotional display which might undermine the denial. It would have been laughable if it had not been so serious. All those weeks scared they would discover where he had been the night Mary Cross died and now they had hauled him in to ask about a different murder.

He wondered how soon he should ask for a solicitor, and whether the very asking might not strengthen Welford's opinion that he was the murderer. *Murderer.* The word rang in his mind as he listened for Welford's next question; it reverberated as it had done years ago when it had been screamed at him across a courtroom. Welford would know. Welford would have been through the records and he would know that Dale had once stood in the dock.

Dale counted only three people who were aware he had been to Benfield on Friday: Al Lomax, the Reverend Adam King and his interfering wife. He deduced that the police had heard from the Kings. 'I went to the vicarage,' he said. 'I wanted to see Mrs King but got the vicar.'

Welford let him explain the visit, both of them knowing that Jenny and the vicar had already told their version. Dale did not stray from the facts. Then Welford said: 'But you weren't with the vicar all the time, were you, Mr Dale? Didn't you tell him you'd wait on your own in the church until his wife got home?' When Dale agreed Welford asked: 'What did you do while you waited?'

Dale shrugged. 'Hung around. Looked around. There wasn't anything to do. After a bit I gave up and went home.'

'Did you go into the vestry? Look in any drawers? Anything like that?'

A shake of the head. Dale could not see where this was leading. The papers said the girl and been found dead in the church but that was a full week after his visit.

There were other questions about what he had seen there but Welford finally appeared to accept that the light was poor and Dale had not noticed anything remarkable. What on earth, Dale demanded, was he supposed to have seen? Three days before the girl went missing? A week before her body was found? Welford did not answer these questions and switched to talking about the night Mary Cross was killed.

Here we go, thought Dale, his stomach tightening. Everything he had feared was becoming real. The police computer had shown up the discrepancies in his answers at the checkpoints, his comings and goings had attracted attention and the next thing would be that his alibi for the night was challenged.

Welford said: 'You've claimed you were in Sheffield when Mary was murdered.'

'Yes.' Dale said he had visited a Brigges factory and stayed overnight.

'You said you were there for two nights, at the Olden Mill Hotel?'

Dale hid the truth a shade longer to find out how much Welford knew, how much the police were guessing. Welford said that a man who looked like Dale and drove the same type of car had been seen on the Harpury road late on 17 May. Was Dale certain of his dates? Might he not have gone to Sheffield another time?'

'I go every few months,' said Dale. 'I'm sure I was there then.'

The fingers of Welford's right hand slowly clenched into a loose fist lying on the polished surface. 'You've been asked about this date several times before, Mr Dale. You've had plenty of time to check if you ever had doubts.'

'No doubts,' said Dale. And not much doubt what was coming next either.

'Well, the Olden Mill Hotel has no record of you staying there on the seventeenth. How can you explain that?'

So they had checked. Dale had the sensation of walking on quicksand. With Welford's last answer the footing had become trickier. If he was clever enough he could avoid being sucked in, but if not . . .'

Dale cleared his throat. 'Inspector, the Olden Mill Hotel is expensive. Brigges's pay up without question when I present my expenses. According to my office diary and to the receipts I give the accounts department, I always stay at the Olden Mill. The truth is I often stay somewhere else, somewhere cheaper. Yes, I fiddle the expenses.'

He was afraid he sounded challenging, daring Welford to be shocked by such petty dishonesty. Welford was unconcerned by his tone. He said: 'Now we've disposed of the fiction that you stayed at the Olden Mill, perhaps you would tell me where you were on the night of 17 May.'

And that, Dale explained, was the reason for keeping up the lie about the Olden Mill. He did not remember. He had spent the night of the sixteenth in a hotel in Sheffield but the next night he stopped at a convenient place on the drive south and had not retained the bill because he had a fake Olden Mill receipt ready for Brigges.

A couple of weeks ago Dale would not have bothered with this confession about his routine of fiddled expenses and faked bills. It would have been enough to say he had been at home on the seventeenth and he would have been positive Sheila would back the story, partly because she would not remember confidently enough to contradict him and partly because she accepted his word unquestioningly. But he'd had to face that he could no longer rely on her. Her condition had deteriorated, she was ricocheting from one crisis to another and she was unpredictable. He was safer with his confession.

Welford persisted in trying to get a hotel name out of him for the seventeenth but Dale was adamant he could not remember. Finally Welford said: 'You haven't got an alibi for that night at all, have you, Mr Dale? We've cancelled out the Olden Mill but you can't offer anything else. From what you say you could have been anywhere south of Sheffield. I put it to you that you were in Hertfield. You met Mary Cross.'

'No!'

'You picked her up. She was hitch-hiking and you picked her up.'

'No!'

'And you killed her.'

'No, no!'

'But you were seen, Mr Dale. You were seen and your car

was seen. Right by the gateway to the field where that girl's body was found early next morning, *you were seen.*'

A wasp came through the window and criss-crossed the air. Neither of them flapped at it. Sweat drenched Dale's shirt, the smell of it filled his nostrils. 'No,' he said again, in a broken voice. 'I never met Mary Cross. All you've got are coincidences. Lots of men have brown hair and beards – look how many were stopped at checkpoints along with me. The car's a Brigges's car – look how many office cars are red Fords. I had nothing to do with Mary Cross and you'll never have any serious evidence to suggest I did.'

The voice in his head told him to calm down, keep his tone even.

Welford said: 'This *is* serious, Mr Dale. Don't be under any illusion about that.' He swiped at the wasp, crushing it on the desk. Then: 'Sunday evening. Last Sunday evening. Where were you then?'

Welford ran a stubby finger around the rim of his collar, easing its pressure on his neck. Dale looked thoughtful. He did not need to think: that was the day he had gone to the pub with Lomax and met the dog fight people for the first time. By evening he was alone in the *Angles* office planning his dog and girl spread for a future issue. Then he had been at the Red Cow with Wendy before calling at another pub for food and driving home. He edited the story and said he had met a friend in a Hertfield pub.

The inspector pushed for more detail and Dale told him that the friend was a woman he wanted to model for *Angles* and they had talked about it in the Red Cow. As the police were already investigating the magazine, the admission appeared harmless. The snag was that Welford demanded times and Dale was not capable to giving them. Bit by bit Welford pieced together what Dale had done for the rest of the evening.

'Did you stop anywhere on the way to Harpury once you'd left Hertfield?' Welford asked. Dale remembered stopping once, to relieve himself. 'Where?' Welford asked. When Dale said he would recognize the place again but did not know the name of it Welford took him into a room with a large map on the wall and asked him to point it out.

'There,' said Dale, tapping the map. Welford did not speak for a few seconds and in the silence Dale sensed he had slipped further into the quicksand.

The inspector asked: 'Did you see anybody when you stopped?'

Yes, Dale said. He saw a fire officer's car haring up the main road and turning down the lane to Benfield. He saw fire engines racing after it.

'No one else?'

'No one.'

Welford pulled at his collar again. 'So you were in Ayot wood, Mr Dale, on the evening Susan Dawlish was attacked there.'

Quicksand.

25

The weekenders had not heard about Mrs Pendle's death and came hammering on her door on Saturday morning to say hello. Jeffrey Miles cowered while they prowled outside and went away without shutting the gate. He sneaked a look at them from Mrs Pendle's bedroom: a couple of frisky young dogs without leads, a couple of children fooling around and a couple of adults in shorts and sandals.

Miles suspected they had made regular visits to Mrs Pendle and that he was likely to be disturbed again before they returned to London. He realized he would have to be extra careful not to give indications that the house was occupied. These people did not merely rattle letter boxes, they shouted through windows. A cup on a draining board could be sufficient to give him away.

In the back room again he turned on the radio, twiddling the knob until he got a station which provided news. The battery was getting noticeably weaker by the hour. He had skimmed the shelves in the village shop to see whether batteries were stocked. They were not on display and he had shied away from asking in case the purchase struck anyone as odd. Jenny would have known he did not own a radio.

He turned to the right station and switched the radio off to save power until it was time for the news. Miles was fascinated by Benfield being famous and after the long television item the other night he hoped for more and if not for television coverage then at least for the village to be mentioned on the radio.

Flopping on the bed he looked across the fields towards Ayot St Martin. Horses were rushing about the meadow.

Lapwings alighted near the hedge. He heard the church clock.

Miles grabbed the radio. Reception was so weak that by the time he had found the most favourable direction for the aerial he had missed the headlines. After that his luck improved because there was an interview with the police officer leading the search for the Demon of Benfield. During this item Jeffrey Miles learned that Veronica Long's body had been found.

He was stunned. The superintendent was describing how the vicar had gone into the Dornaye vault in preparation for the funeral on Monday of an elderly woman, one of the last members of a family who had once been influential land-owners in the county. Miles's instinct was to clap his hands over his ears but the gesture was momentary. Compelled to listen, he scooped up the radio, cradling it in his hands and holding it close to his head. He braced himself for the rest. There was a lot about Veronica and a lot more linking her fate to that of Mary Cross and Susan Dawlish.

He crouched beside the bed, tense. Policemen would be in St John's! His work with the carvings would be interrupted. He had no hope that he would be left alone: either they would be watching him or else they would stop him getting on with it at all. And there would be questions. House-to-house questions meant they would go to Pendle Cottage and find him there and he would be made to leave. He ground his teeth. He hated questions! At least when they had made their inquiries about the first dead girl Jenny King had spoken up for him and sworn he was in the vicarage all evening. This time no one would help him and they might not be equally willing to believe him when his story was not corroborated by the vicar's wife.

Miles's panic subsided. The police would be told Pendle Cottage was empty, there was a good chance he would be safe there. He expected to see the police on Monday when he went to work. They could ask him then whatever they liked. No one knew he was at the cottage and unless he gave it away, no one would find out.

He thought about the unexpected news that Mrs Pendle had been a Dornaye and her remains destined for the vault.

For the first time he poked around among the woman's books and papers and found evidence of her pedigree, in a scribbled dedication in one volume and in a faded clipping from *The Times* announcing her marriage to a James Pendle. If he had known that, he thought angrily, he would never have supposed Stan Albury was digging her grave. And he would have completed Jenny King's sentence differently, not jumping to a conclusion about cremation. Jenny had been about to mention interment in the vault.

Carefully, he replaced the things he had disturbed. A moroseness settled on him. Things were going desperately wrong again. Just as the camp had ended in disappointment so had the cottage. Nothing good ever lasted. He tried to cheer himself up by remembering the carvings, the satisfaction of cold stone beneath his hands and the fine work of their creator. Useless. He had lost his pleasure in them and their creator had deserted him.

Next day the neighbours tried the door again. Anybody in the village could have told them Mrs Pendle was dead but they kept themselves to themselves and had not heard. Miles remembered the business of Veronica and the man in the wood and decided he had been wrong to assume it was one of the weekenders. That meant the man was local. The police would have a tough session with him, Miles thought. It was common knowledge that husbands and lovers were prime suspects when women were murdered.

Miles listened to news bulletins and heard that people were coming forward with information about the Demon of Benfield. Otherwise he did nothing but watch light change over the fields. Despite his outward listlessness he felt himself gearing up for a move. In a short while he would leave Benfield. He had left other places easily enough and what was precious about Benfield now that he had accepted the carvings meant nothing to him?

26

Marion Knox, Pauline Williams and Ralph Gough were in a gossipy huddle in the press officer's office on Monday morning. Roger Dale had not turned up for work and the papers said a Hertfordshire man had been helping the police with their inquiries over the weekend. Unable to contain the secret any longer Marion had told Gough about the letter from a Veronica Long offering to model. When Pauline joined them they were well into speculation about Dale's guilt but this time they were half in earnest.

'You should have gone to the police, Pauline,' Marion chided. 'Now Veronica Long's dead too.' She affected the little pout Ruth James made whenever the script called for her to tell anyone: 'I told you so'.

Pauline did not say she had telephoned the police on Saturday. It would do nothing to remove Marion's censure because the call had been too late to save Veronica Long. The police who visited Pauline at her flat on Saturday evening had not criticized her. They had seemed glad of her information. All Sunday she had pictured Dale being snatched away from his wife and children on her say so.

Pauline reminded Marion: 'It appears the police have got someone.'

Gough ran a hand over his crinkly hair and said, his Scots accent exaggerated by excitement: 'It appears they've got Roger Dale. He's normally here hours before this.'

Marion chipped in that Pauline ought to telephone Dale's home and ask whether he was coming in. 'Then we could find out the truth.'

Pauline came nearer laughter than she had done all

weekend. 'How? You want me to ask Mrs Dale whether her husband is down at the police station being charged with a couple of murders?'

Marion gave a wriggle of impatience. 'Oh, you know, Pauline. There are more subtle ways than that.'

Marion was seldom subtle herself. Gough, knowing it, gave Pauline the slightest wink. 'All right,' he said to Marion. 'Let's ring Mrs Dale and find out – subtly. But *you* do it. You can pretend Pauline is off sick today and I need to contact Roger.' While an astonished Marion was marshalling her objections Roger Dale arrived.

Dale made a great effort to carry on normally. He had much to do and found it difficult to concentrate because his mind was full of the weekend's events. The police had allowed him home on Saturday but that had not been the end of it. Next day they had come for him again. His car had been taken away for examination and he had endured hours more questioning about the attacks on the three women.

He had clung to his story about the unremembered hotel on the night Mary Cross died because an eye-witness report that he was at the scene was apparently the strongest evidence linking him with any of the crimes. Giving up that alibi would make it even more difficult to persuade Welford he was innocent.

After all those hours of persistent questions Dale had a fair idea how little the police had against him. Quite possibly they would never have suspected him of attacking Susan Dawlish but for his sheer bad luck in mentioning he had been in Ayot wood. The fire officer had reported seeing a man run from the trees and drive away erratically in a red car but had given no description. Veronica's acquisition of *Angles* and Dale's visit to the church where her corpse was found were all the police had to connect him with her.

He caught himself staring vacantly across the office and registered the serious expression on his secretary's face. He would have to get rid of her. Once this police business was over he would make a fresh effort to have her replaced. There was a woman on the sixth floor he would much prefer.

When Pauline went to lunch he took her newspaper and

read the report on the murder inquiries. There was a strong suggestion that the man who had been at Hertfield police station over the weekend would prove to be the Demon of Benfield. The police had sounded confident enough for the reporter to slant the piece that way.

The paper was not the one delivered to his home, the one Sheila had been reading when he left. That one also indicated that the killer had been caught and Sheila's relief was palpable. She had slept badly for several nights, fretting that the house would not be secure until the new window was fitted.

So far she had swallowed his story about visiting the police station because of a traffic accident, although she was indignant that it should be taking up so much of his time. How long would it be before she realized the real reason the police wanted him?

He dropped Pauline's paper on her desk as the telephone rang. Lomax. 'Roger, what the hell's going on?' Lomax was using that clipped way of speaking which came when he was tense.

Dale supposed someone in Hertfield had recognized him being taken into the police station. Or perhaps an indiscreet policeman had let his name slip?

Before Dale spoke Lomax went on: 'I'm in the office. Back numbers are missing and the subscriptions list has vanished. Someone has been hunting around in here.'

Dale said he had removed the things himself. 'I took a lot of stuff home. I want to go through some back numbers one evening.'

'Oh. But what about the subscriptions list?' The tone had relaxed.

'I must have gathered that up by mistake. I'll look tonight. You don't need it, do you, Al?'

Lomax said not. Then: 'There's another of those . . . er . . . events tonight. Coming?'

Dale said yes and Lomax told him which pub to meet him at. Dale asked: 'What about Havoc? Have you decided whether to buy?'

'I want to talk to you about that,' said Lomax and rang off.

The next time the telephone rang it was the security man in the entrance hall to say there were two gentlemen to see him. Dale asked what they wanted but they had given only their names and those conveyed nothing. With misgivings Dale took the lift to the ground floor. When the doors opened he was facing two plain-clothes policemen.

He almost jabbed the button and sent the lift zooming away from them. He controlled the instinct. If they had come for him, then he had to go. There was no possibility of dodging them and an attempt to do so would be as strong an indication of his guilt as anything they already had. Dale tightened his jaw and walked forward to meet them. His legs felt weak, as though the marble floor yielded at every step.

27

It was not until Monday morning that the vicar remembered to talk to Jenny about Jeffrey Miles and the carvings. Police had taken over the church and had use of a room in the vicarage too. Everything centred on Veronica's death and medieval carvings were of no consequence. The sight of Miles crossing the churchyard reminded King.

Jenny looked stupefied when he told her how the work had become haphazard and the carvings damaged. Then she suggested Miles's impatience to find out what lay beneath each panel could mean his next job was awaiting him. Had he not said something about taking on a project in the West Country?

Her husband said: 'He mentioned it once, weeks ago. You'd think he'd have told us if his time here was running out.'

She went back to cutting bread for toast. 'Oh, well, you know Jeff. He doesn't say more than he's forced to, does he?'

King sounded exasperated. 'No, I *don't* know Jeffrey Miles. I don't think any of us really know him.'

Jenny laughed. 'Adam, he likes it that way. You've been telling me so for weeks. Likes to keep himself to himself and so on. I'm the one who's been trying to draw him out – remember?'

She dropped two slices of bread into the toaster, deciding to protect Miles's privacy and not share with Adam the secret that Jeff was living at Pendle Cottage. There was too much risk he would pass it on to the police and they might go round there even though they could talk to Miles at the church any time.

Jenny calculated that he had not been living at the cottage

when Veronica disappeared. He had been away from the village, if not actually in Harpury, and consequently could be of no interest to the police. She saw no excuse for having him upset by needless questions. The carvings, though, were different. 'You'd better ask him what's going on,' she told Adam. 'And you can do it now. He's coming over here.'

Tactfully she withdrew in case Miles thought the Kings were ganging up against him. She put her head into the big room Miles had once used and where the police had based themselves for as long as they needed to be in the village. No one was in there but one of the vicarage cats had curled up on a chair. She did not bother to chase it out because the long window was pushed up and the animal could run straight back in.

In the kitchen the Reverend Adam King was wishing his wife had not deserted him. He had not had time to ask her to deal with Miles and now he had to cope himself. Miles tapped at the back door and walked in. 'The police say I can't go into the church yet,' he said.

'You know what happened there?' King was considering taking the easy way out and asking the police to keep Miles away altogether. But that would not solve the difficulty. The time would still arrive when King had to say something about the carvings. As he opened his mouth to begin the bread flew out of the toaster.

Miles said: 'It was on the radio. About Veronica Long.'

King ignored the toast and poured Miles a mug of tea. He used the nearest clean mug. Miles said: 'Jenny always give me the other one.'

'Oh.' King tipped the tea into the prettier mug. He was struggling to find an opening which would not be schoolmasterly but when the pause had lengthened he felt obliged to say something to get the subject going. 'I've been inspecting the carvings, Jeffrey, and . . . well, I wonder whether you aren't fed up with the work.'

He hesitated but Miles only watched, unflinching. King floundered on. 'What I mean is you seem to be dashing at the panels now. The first ones were perfect but the more recent ones . . . In fact, I counted quite a few scratches.'

It was maddening the way Miles said nothing, just held him in that grey-eyed gaze. King said: 'And a chip. St Michael's wing is definitely chipped.' Another pause. No response. King summed up: 'The point is, I'd rather you didn't carry on if it's become a bore and the carvings are suffering.'

Behind his icy exterior Miles was wounded. Of course he had been conscious of his eagerness to unmask the subjects but he had intended to backtrack and finish each panel thoroughly. He really believed he had intended that. And he had never realized his speed had caused damage.

A policeman came into the kitchen and King introduced him to Miles. It was a good opportunity, the officer said, to ask him a few questions. Miles was invited to the makeshift office and asked to recall who and what he had seen in St John's around the time Veronica disappeared.

When they left the kitchen King picked up a piece of toast. It was cold. He slammed it down on the table and went to his study without breakfast.

Miles repeated the lie about living in Harpury. He had no hesitation because almost the first thing the police officer said to him was: 'Mrs King says you live in Harpury. That's right, is it?'

Miles cited the times of the buses he claimed to use travelling back and forth. Then he was asked about events on the day Veronica vanished. He told how the Arthur Bellerman Society had explored the church and how the girl brought his afternoon tea. He omitted the part about leaving the platform and talking to her and said she put the tea down in a pew for him to collect. Shortly after, he said, a man opened the church door and she went out with him. Miles said he had not glimpsed the man.

'But you're sure it was a man?' the officer asked.

'I heard his voice. He had an American accent.'

The officer did not explain that the man had already been traced because while Veronica was officially missing the vicar had reported her flirtation. The man with the facsimile confirmed meeting her and said they sat outside the church while he showed her his book. He had not been out of his companions' sight for the next few days and Veronica had been alive and well much later on the day he had talked to her.

Miles wished he could walk away through the open window and over the lawn to the wood. Then he would feel protected. But he could not move. He had to stay and answer questions. The officer asked him about the time Susan Dawlish was attacked. As it had happened on a Sunday evening Miles just reminded him he was in Benfield only on weekdays.

There followed a rather general chat about the church, about the way the Kings kept keys in the vestry allowing everyone access to everything. Miles remembered King once telling him he preferred to leave them available than have locks smashed, because if people were determined to get in anywhere they could always do so. He quoted the vicar.

Miles understood the session to be no more than routine because the radio news that morning suggested the search was over. He wanted to ask whether the suspect who had been at the police station was Veronica's lover but knew he had better not reveal any special interest. He asked instead how soon he could get back to work.

'I'll ask about that,' the policeman said, 'but I shouldn't think there'll be any reason to keep you out.' He got up, indicating the end of the interview.

Miles went to the church. There was nowhere else to go. He was smarting after King's criticism and did not want to stay in the vicarage. At the church another police officer, with a young and acned face above his uniform, told him the Pendle funeral had been delayed because of the murder. The constable was excited to be on a murder inquiry, a change from the petty day-to-day things for which he usually qualified. Even though he was being used as a mere security guard to keep unauthorized people out of St John's he felt quite important.

'They reckon they've got the chap, you know, the so-called Demon,' he confided to Miles as he confided to most people he encountered. 'They had him in and out of Hertfield police station all weekend.'

'Why do they let him go?'

'What? Oh, well, I don't know. I'm stuck up here, aren't I? But I'd say they know he's the one but they've got to build up the case a bit before they charge him. If their evidence isn't firm enough a jury could acquit, no matter how guilty he is.'

Once Miles got permission to work, the constable talked up to him on the platform. When the man wasn't speaking the rhythm of his tread, from the porch to the plaque to the fallen and back again, was a background to Miles's work.

Miles knelt by the basilisk, fondling the crested form, as he strove to evoke emotions it had previously released in him. But all he felt was intense guilt at breaking faith with the medieval craftsman whose treasures had been entrusted to him. His punishment was the loss of joy.

28

The men who drove Dale to Hertfield from London were taciturn. At the station Inspector Welford asked new questions which related more to *Angles* than to murderous assaults. Through these questions Dale gathered that Travis had discovered he was responsible for one of the suspect box-number advertisements and the sergeant had also spotted the one where he had used Brigges's address.

'Who', asked Welford wearing a tight-necked shirt of another colour, 'answered these advertisements?'

'No one. I put them in sometimes to fill up the column. There usually aren't any replies.'

'What about Veronica Long?'

'No. I keep telling you. I've never had a letter from anyone in Benfield.'

'You say you take most of the photographs for the magazine, Mr Dale. Would you mind telling me where you get your models?' Welford was commendably polite but did not disguise his determination. He sat, big hands relaxed on the desk top between them, and listened.

Dale told him. The admission seemed harmless because the girls did what they did quite freely. Suddenly Dale was being asked about a Miss Sandra Sutton who had been with him in his car when he was stopped at a checkpoint. He got that feeling of being on quicksand. 'Where is she now?' Welford asked.

'I've no idea. She caught a train home. To Manchester.' Dale tried not to sound aggressive but sheer tension made him defiant.

'No, Mr Dale. Young Sandra hasn't been home since she

made her trip to London to visit a model agency. Her mother's reported her missing. I thought you might be able to help us trace her.'

Dale insisted too loudly that he knew nothing. Welford said calmly: 'I'm sure you appreciate why I asked. She was seen with you in the Hertfield area – the area where Mary Cross and Veronica Long were found dead and someone tried to kill Susan Dawlish. I suppose you'll want me to believe it's just another coincidence.'

By evening Dale had apparently succeeded because he was handed his car keys and allowed to leave. He drove as far as the *Angles* office and telephoned Sheila. His wife, he had frequently reminded the police, was in a delicate nervous state and not to be upset. He hoped they had taken his word and not been to the house while he was away.

Sheila sounded no worse than before, even though her mother had telephoned again fussing about her safety with a killer around. He told her he had to work late. His facility for separating the strands of his life had saved him from a miserable evening at home worrying about Welford. All that interested him now was getting to the pub in time to meet Lomax.

He went fast, missed a turning and had to go back, wasted more time in badly signposted lanes and stopped to look at a map. Then he roared off again.

Lomax's car was swinging out of the car park. Dale flashed his lights and followed. The other men had already gone. Lomax streaked along the lanes with Dale close behind. They had to cross a major road and Lomax got over but Dale waited for a column of lorries to trundle by. When he got across, Lomax had gone.

Dale went at speed expecting to sight Lomax's tail lights around a bend but there was nothing. He was growing doubtful, afraid he had overlooked an entrance but unable to remember so much as an open field gate. Approaching houses, he searched to left and right. Then the hamlet was behind him and he was nearing a farm, a dilapidated place. Through its ragged hedge he saw glinting metal. Dale pulled up beside Lomax's car.

'You took your time,' said Lomax.

'Delayed at the office.'

They entered a barn. The scene was much the same as before but without the opulence. Dale's blood coursed faster. A scruffy man brought brandies across. Dale and Lomax placed bets on the big fight, eyeing the contestants like connoisseurs.

Lomax spoke from the corner of his mouth. 'Roger, before this gets too lively I want to talk to you about Havoc.' There was no enthusiasm in his voice.

Dale said: 'You're not going ahead, then? Have you told Rex?'

'Not yet. And I'm not going to tell him the reasons, either.'

'You're not convinced about the pedigree? I don't blame you. It's only his word, isn't it?'

Lomax said that was about it. Then: 'Havoc isn't the only animal. I want to choose a pup. If it's from the right stock I don't mind waiting for it to grow up.'

'Expensive,' murmured Dale. He had learned a lot about the dogs, including the cost, and he knew only one way Lomax could raise the money: sell his interest in *Angles*.

Lomax sketched a line in the dust of the barn floor with a scuffed shoe. 'I'd need a partner,' he said. 'I'd rather choose him, too. What do you say, Roger?'

'Sell off *Angles*?' suggested Dale.

Lomax smiled cautiously. 'Could you bear that?'

'Oh, yes,' said Dale. What had been unthinkable days ago was now the best way out. *Angles* had become trouble. The fun was over. Time for something else.

'Good,' said Lomax. 'We'll look around for a buyer.'

Dale said they could probably sell to a man at the printers' who had always shown interest in it. Lomax smiled again. He tossed back his drink and fetched more. 'New ventures,' he said and they raised their glasses to the death of *Angles* and the future of the American pit.

The first fight was an uncourageous effort. 'Beginners,' sneered Rex who had sidled close to Lomax to press him about Havoc.

Lomax wiped his mouth on the back of a freckled hand. He

was about to tell Rex the deal was off when a burly man dragging a dog brushed by. Dale was open-mouthed as he recognized Mrs Catesby's Rusty.

Rusty's attention was on the other dogs. He was quivering. His ears drooped abjectly. Rex joked with the burly man: 'That thing's got no chance. Do you expect anyone to bet on that?'

The man laughed. 'You only breed a fighter by letting him win, Rex.'

Anticipation sickened Dale. Within minutes Rusty was forced into the ring. A pit was unleashed on him. Dale gulped down his brandy and looked away. He avoided the sight of the old dog's ripped flesh but the stench of faeces and hot blood could not be shut out, nor the screams. Dale heard him being slaughtered, slowly, agonizingly and purely to let a pit experience the triumph of another dog's death.

Nobody was going to intervene to save Rusty as they would a real fighting animal. The purpose of this spectacle was for him to be killed. Through Dale's mind flashed Mrs Catesby and her useless offer of a reward for Rusty's return. She had been right about the dog being stolen. None of the men would allow a dog they owned to be destroyed in this fashion. They would steal one.

Dale felt his gorge rising. He had seen anonymous dogs savaged in the ring but Rusty had growled through his garden fence and been his neighbour's pet. It wasn't at all the same thing.

As the excitement reached a crescendo Dale opened his eyes and saw the pit tossing the corpse. Simultaneously he saw the barn door open and the police appear.

Men ran, desperate for a way out. To Dale's horror Rex, close to him, fired a gun in the direction of the door. The burly man tackled Rex, bringing him down. Someone else kicked the gun and sent it spinning across the floor to rest in the ring, in the blood. Everyone was shouting, no one's words distinct. All Dale understood for certain was that the police were armed too.

Dale was led out. The rest were to be in the barn some time answering questions about the dog fights but the police wanted him for murder.

At the police station Inspector Welford faced him once more. 'We've got some nosy men on the roads tonight, Mr Dale. When they saw you tearing across the county away from home and Harpury they were curious enough to follow you. I reckon this is going to be my lucky evening.'

Welford opened a folder on the polished desk. 'Sandra Sutton,' he said and held up prints of the girl with the upturned nose. 'Pity about that appendix scar.'

Dale did not respond. Welford said: 'Where were they taken? Not at the *Angles* office, I know. We've had a good look at that and there isn't a bed in sight. Oh, by the way, it'll be a waste of time denying you took these pictures.' He held up the sheet of contacts, indicating the one where Sandra posed against a mirror and Dale had photographed his own reflection.

Dale said they were taken when he was last in Manchester. Welford preferred to believe they were shot in Hertfield when Dale drove her there after she went to his London office. Pauline Williams filled Dale's mind. *She* must have told the police because no one else knew about Sandra Sutton's visit. He hated Pauline Williams.

Welford produced something else from the folder, the letter Veronica Long had written to Dale. He read it out, stressing the bit about her having no objection to nude modelling and the details of her measurements. 'This was at the *Angles* office too. Caught up with other papers in a drawer. So now we know for sure, don't we, Mr Dale?'

Dale gaped at the letter, barely listening to Welford saying the address on it was that of Veronica's friend in London. He was hunting for a way out. Welford's wisps of circumstantial evidence had become a web.

The room was hot. He felt he was suffocating. A desperate anger built up inside him, boiled over. He cracked. *'I haven't killed anybody!'*

Welford did not flinch. He looked him in the eye. 'Never, Mr Dale?'

Sweat was running down Dale's face. 'That was different,' he said, reduced to a mumble. 'That was a long time ago.'

'Never is even longer.'

'It wasn't at all the same thing,' Dale protested in a broken voice.

'You drove a car at a woman. You were drunk. You'd had a row with her because she rejected you and you drove a car at her. A car can be a lethal weapon, Mr Dale. What you did was a violent act. You aren't, I hope, going to tell me you can't be a violent man.'

Dale groaned. His hands cupped his ears but Welford's voice was relentless. 'What happened to Mary Cross? Did you pick her up when she was hitch-hiking and kill her when she refused to have sex with you? And Susan Dawlish? Didn't you see her walking home to Ayot St Martin and follow her into the trees. And Veronica Long? Didn't you kill her in Benfield wood . . .'

Dale snapped that he thought Veronica was found dead in St John's. Welford said yes, so she was, but she was murdered in the wood. Leaf mould and other debris on the body showed she had been killed there and concealed in the church later.

'You'd taken to meeting her in the wood, hadn't you?' Welford said in the same insistent way. 'We know she used to meet a married man there some evenings. It would be quite convenient for you on your way to Harpury from the *Angles* office, wouldn't it?'

A light in the police station car park went out revealing how dark the night had become. Dale's world shrank to one bleak room. No sight of anything else. No sound except Welford's calm breath while he waited for Dale to confess.

Dale's memory fled back through the years to a similar room when a sheet of paper had been set in front of him and he had written the words which led to other small rooms before the contrasting space of a courtroom where a barrister argued that he'd had a stainless character until then. The speech was a good one and everyone said he got off lightly because he was not sent to prison for very long.

Welford went away leaving Dale to think. Panicking, Dale could see himself losing everything he had achieved since. He was a family man now and Sheila knew no more about that business than she did about *Angles* or his other women.

If the Benfield murders got him into court she would learn everything. Sheila could never survive the strain and the stigma. She would leave and take the children with her. He detested the unfairness of it. Oh, he had been careless and over confident about *Angles* and deceiving girls with talk of modelling careers, but to be accused of *murder* . . .'

Down the corridor Welford met Inspector Addison and young Travis. 'Not long now,' said Welford, trying not to be smug.

Addison beamed. 'And he's already delivered the dog-fighting crowd to us. Not a bad night's work.'

Young Travis said something surprising. 'Why weren't the girls sexually assaulted? From what we know of Dale's tastes it's strange none of them were.'

29

Jenny King decided to speak to Jeffrey Miles about her plan to enable him to stay at the cottage. She believed his unhappy state derived from uncertainty about his future there and she regretted telling the police he lived in Harpury. Both she and Miles would have easier consciences when the truth was known.

On Monday afternoon she got as far as saying she needed to talk to him but was called away. After that she drove to Hertfield to leave her car at the garage for the mechanics to start work on it first thing next day.

Miles settled down for another evening in Back Lane. The radio battery was almost exhausted but he heard the news. There was nothing fresh about the Demon of Benfield. He concentrated then on the carvings, calculating how long it would take to finish the panels. Penitent about his previous mistreatment of them, he was now being scrupulous although this meant very slow work and he wanted to be on his way. Soon he must revive the story about another job waiting for him in the West Country and then disappear from Benfield as abruptly as he had come.

He listened to larks above the fields while he wondered where to go next. Perhaps he would not work with stone any more although he did enjoy it and had accumulated knowledge it would be a pity to waste. Just for a spell, perhaps, he would try something else. He could not think what. A holiday first, maybe. He'd had periods when he did not work, when he was ill, but he had not had a holiday since childhood. And those holidays had been noisy and energetic occasions with his boisterous family, quite unlike anything that appealed to him. He was glad he had cut himself off from his family.

He guessed he would have sufficient money to take a holiday because the vicar was going to pay him a final lump of the agreed sum when he finished. Wales sounded attractive, with its mountains and its emptiness. He thought he might go there.

A noise at the front door had him on his feet, apprehensive. Miles tiptoed to the top of the stairs. He could see down the passage. The letter box was being rattled. He waited for the sound to stop but when it did the caller did not walk away. The worst happened. He heard Jenny King's voice.

'Jeff?' she called softly. 'I know you're there. Open the door.'

Next she was squinting up at him through the letter box. He was livid. He ran downstairs and tugged open the door. 'What do you want?'

'I must talk to you, Jeff. Let me come in.'

She did not give him any choice because she stepped forward as she spoke and he recoiled to prevent her bare forearm brushing against his. He waited for her to explain herself but he had made up his mind about the underlying reason for her visit. Incurable nosiness.

Jenny went ahead of him into the back sitting room. Miles suspected her of checking he had not damaged or stolen anything. She said: 'I know you've been living here. I thought you'd be happier if it was above board and Mrs Pendle's nephew let you stay until you've finished at the church.' She did not want his gratitude but she had no idea how he wilfuly misinterpreted her every word and gesture.

Miles caught his breath. He could not believe the extent of her interference and he definitely did not want it known where he was living. 'No,' he said but she misunderstood his reasons and rushed on to say she was sure she could arrange it so he did not have to pay rent.

He grasped she was talking about plans, not something she had set in motion. There was a chance of dissuading her. 'No,' he said again. 'I'll leave. I'll go somewhere else. Harpury. I'll go back to Harpury.'

Jenny laughed, tried to lighten his anxiety. Her laughter offended. She made it plain she was willing to approach the family for him. 'Leave it to me, Jeff. It'll be all right. I'm sure it will. I've got to telephone the nephew tonight about a new date for the funeral. I'll mention it then.'

He asked who else knew he was at the cottage. Jenny crossed her heart. 'Not a soul, I promise. Not even Adam. I haven't breathed a word. I wanted to talk to you first.'

Oh yes, Miles seethed. She wanted to talk, always to talk but never to listen. She was not listening now to him telling her to mind her own business.

Apologizing for disturbing him, she went to the front door. He was panic stricken. Jenny was speaking but in Miles's head her words were jumbled, she might have been saying anything. He took up one of Mrs Pendle's walking sticks and followed her down the path.

Anger hampered his breathing. Jenny would not leave him alone. She never had. But there was worse. She had guessed he was never at Harpury, laughing when he said he would go back there. Jenny must be aware he was in Benfield when Veronica was killed. It was essential she told nobody he was at the cottage. Not the Pendle nephew, nor the vicar, nor the police. No one.

But then Miles pictured her car parked by the hedge. Numb he watched her walking away from him, turning to wave and walking away. His grip tightened on the stick and then he flung it down. He could not drive. Her car would be stuck outside Pendle Cottage until someone found it while looking for her. If he did what he felt compelled to do he would have to leave the cottage immediately after because the car would prove she had been there. He was impotent. He had to allow Jenny to get away from him and spoil everything.

Dully he reached the end of the front path. Something quite unexpected happened. Jenny trotted up the lane. *She had not come by car!* Miles looked wildly round. He snatched up the broken stave that had never been fixed back on the gate and once she was out of sight around the curve of the lane he ran after her, very fast.

He understood precisely what she would do. She would

run as far as the stile and get into the wood. Without her car it was the shortest route home. Miles bounded at the steep bank and scrambled up into the wood. He knew it so well he could tell where their paths would converge.

In St John's the Reverend Adam King was mourning the loss of the atmosphere the building had acquired through seven centuries of prayer. The hideous discovery in the vault ruined it for him. The church of which he was so proud to be incumbent was sullied. He doubted he would ever enter it again without recalling the ghastly moment when he shone his torch among the coffins. He had been struck dumb but Stan Albury had given tongue to every blasphemy the old fellow had in his vocabulary.

King was seriously thinking that perhaps Jenny had been right about a city parish. Dreadful things went on in cities too but was it not possible they hit one less hard for being half expected?

The visitors' book caught his eye. Oh dear, he thought. Visitors. In future there would be more than ever and not because of his wonderful carvings or Arthur Bellerman or the Dornaye memorials. It would be prurient interest in the scene of a murder. He turned the pages of the book, thinking that because of the tragedy entries would soar in next year's pages. Then he tut-tutted in the way Jenny called old maidish when she heard him do it.

'Something wrong, sir?' asked the spotty young constable coming in from the porch and eager for any excuse to fall into conversation.

King pointed to the page. 'Somebody's crossed out an entry. Quite messily.'

The constable did not regard this as a major disaster. 'I thought people usually wrote things in. Silly things like Mickey Mouse or Kilroy Was Here.'

'They do. There's a Kilroy on the next page,' said King treating the constable's remark with undue seriousness.

The young man picked up the book. Inquisitive and with little to do he carried it out into the porch for better light, saying: 'I wonder what it was they decided to hide?'

The vicar was not interested. The matter was a trivial irritation and he rather wished the police would swap the constable for one who made his presence less obvious. Then his head jerked up as he heard the constable swear.

The spotty face was alight with excitement. 'I think I'd better hold on to this, sir,' he said importantly and ran down the path.

King was on his tail. He caught up near the back door of the vicarage. 'What the hell is it?' King demanded, surprising himself with his lapse.

The constable did not notice. 'See for yourself.' He held out the book.

Through the marks of a thick blue felt pen words in black ballpoint were visible. The date was 17 May. The name was Mary Cross.

30

In the vicarage an austere detective inspector and his sergeant were describing their interview with Sheila Dale. The sergeant said they had tried their best but Mrs Dale collapsed and they had to fetch a neighbour, a Mrs Catesby, to sit with her when they left.

'It was the spaceman that did it,' she said. 'Up until then she was telling us Roger couldn't have had anything to do with those women's deaths. But once we showed her a plastic toy similar to the one found near Mary Cross's body she keeled over. Her six-year-old son owns one and the whole family has been searching for it for weeks. She was positive she'd last seen it in the family car.'

Just then the constable and the vicar burst into the room with the visitors' book. The inspector was convinced. 'She must have been here before Mrs King saw her at the southernmost Benfield turn.'

He telephoned his superior in Hertfield. 'Looks as though we might have something else to link Dale to these killings. Mary Cross visited St John's where Veronica's body was dumped.'

He explained the rest and then: 'There's a chap working in the church all day and he doesn't miss much. He was very helpful about the people who came in and out around the time Veronica was killed. Perhaps he can dredge up a memory of Mary Cross being in there.'

Two men were sent to see Miles. The chatty constable remembered his duties and locked the church. The vicar dithered. Jenny was late back from the garage. A telephone rang. The officer who took the call said it was for her.

King explained her absence. The woman sergeant interjected: 'Oh no, she didn't miss the bus from Hertfield. We saw her near Ayot crossroads and offered her a lift home but she said she had to make a quick visit on the way.'

King went to his study to read until she came. He had a shrewd idea she had gone to Pendle Cottage. For the life of him he could not think why. There was no one there and no business which could not wait.

In a while he heard the telephone again but nobody referred the call to him. He wished they would charge the man the news reports said was at the police station and the sooner the better. Then the vicarage could get back to normal. For one thing his telephone would once more be plugged into the socket in his study instead of in the spare room. The parish could get back to normal too. There had been some fuss about Veronica going with a married man although it had been furiously denied.

King thought it very unfortunate the poor fellow's name had been besmirched by unfounded rumour and wondered how long it would be before the foolish accusations were forgotten and the young husband's reputation restored. Longer, he expected, than it would take for Susan Dawlish to recover. The hospital said she was improving and King supposed it would be his duty to call on her once she was fit to receive visitors.

He heard his name and looked out into the passage. The woman sergeant was there, puzzled. 'That address we've got for Jeffrey Miles doesn't exist, Mr King. The officers on their way to Harpury have an up-to-date map in the car but say the street Miles gave isn't on it. Of course, we might have taken it down wrongly from him . . .'

'No,' said King with sudden conviction. 'No, I don't think you did. I think he was being secretive. He never tells anyone more than he thinks they need to know.'

He went with her and repeated this for her colleagues, adding: 'My wife probably knows where he lives but I'm afraid I can't help.'

'Well, how much longer is her "quick visit" going to last?' asked the inspector. He wanted to get to Miles quickly. When the people of Benfield were asked two months ago about Mary Cross the police had not suggested she might have been in the church. Getting Miles to concentrate on it might trigger recollections. It was not impossible he had seen her with Dale that day.

The inspector understood how impatient they were getting in Hertfield. Welford sensed he was close to a confession but that did not necessarily mean he would get one. A second eye-witness account to connect Dale with the Cross murder could mean the difference between charging him or having to let him go when the legal time limit for holding him was reached.

King shook his head. 'I can never tell how long my wife will be. But I can guess where she is.'

'Good,' said the inspector and made for the door. 'We'll go straight there.' King had to tag behind him giving directions.

The inspector and the sergeant drove to Back Lane. When they had gone another officer interrupted King to say he needed to go to the cottage too. He did not have transport and asked the best way on foot. King gave up. He was going to get no reading done, that was obvious. 'There's a short cut,' he said. 'I'll take you.'

Dale struggled for his calmest tone. 'There are thousands of those toys. I can't say whether this one's my son's.'

'No, perhaps you can't,' said Welford, 'but I dare say our forensic chaps could. Carpet fluff in the crevices? A speck of something to prove it's been in your car? That bit of rag . . .'

'All right. *All right!* The rag's meant to be a scarf. My daughter tied it there.'

Welford was certain then there would be a confession, the Mary Cross killing first and the others to follow. Afterwards he would let Dale know that Sandra Sutton had turned up alive and well and was answering questions about his activities as a photographer. But Dale confessed only to lying about 17 May.

He could have stuck it out but the damage was done. Sheila had told the police about Timothy's spaceman and in return they had explained why her husband was being held. He had nothing left to protect. Not *Angles*. Not his family.

Dale told the whole truth knowing as he had known from the very beginning that it would not be accepted. He said he had gone to Hertfield on the night of the murder to work on *Angles* and met a friend. When he started driving home he discovered he was too drunk and turned round in a field entrance. He urinated by the hedge and then, before moving on, polished the car windscreen where moths and other insects were splattered.

'I remember taking a cloth from the door pocket and some bits and pieces coming out with it, garage receipts and a pair of sunglasses,' he said. 'I suppose the spaceman fell out too but I put the rest back and never noticed. Then I went to the *Angles* office and slept in the chair.'

The inspector failed to disguise his eager look. Dale disappointed him. 'I didn't see any girl, dead or alive. The first I knew about a murder was next morning when I heard it on the radio.'

Welford expected to charge him within the hour.

Miles saw the flash of magenta. A fury burned within him as he waited to pounce. Trees blurred. His vision dimmed and he saw only the brilliant garment drawing closer. Jenny was making a noise, her footsteps thudding on the drought-dry path and her bracelet jangling as she bounded along. He held his breath and chose his time.

He meant to strike immediately she passed him. She would not have space to turn, he would be so fast. Mary Cross had not had time, nor had Veronica Long. Susan Dawlish would not have escaped either if the lad shooting pigeons had not chosen that instant to fire his gun making her jerk away and Miles land a glancing blow.

A rabbit came on to the path. Jenny stopped rather than frighten it. As it loped away she took a step. She faltered. She had a peculiar feeling something was wrong. What? She identified the feeling. She was not alone. Somebody was watching her. Fear tingled her spine.

Jenny whirled round, checking for a presence, human or animal. She saw nothing but trees and ran forward again, alert.

The incident had put Miles off. His moment was missed, he had let her get ahead of him. Cutting through scrub oaks he headed for another point where he could appear alongside the path.

Jenny ran on, glancing back frequently. She was positive there had been someone near her, on her left. She considered leaving the wood and taking the path, but that lay to her left and it was possible the other person would use it too. A path with a wood on one side, a field on the other and a graveyard at the end of it was no safer than the place she was in. She would be wiser to move to her right and join the woodland path from the village green to the church. Other people were likely to be in that direction and other people were the greatest deterrent to an attacker.

Miles got way in front of her. After taking up position he decided there was better cover further over and crossed to the right side of the path. Listening hard, he was surprised not to hear Jenny coming towards him. Breaking twigs some way off puzzled him until he realized she was heading for the main path. He scuttled after her.

Jenny was cursing her favourite outfit for its inability to camouflage her. Each time she paused she heard someone moving through the undergrowth. If he would come out and fight she would be a match for him. But Mary Cross and Susan Dawlish and Veronica Long had not had a chance. They had all been battered from behind. Jenny calmed herself and put her predicament into another perspective. The police had caught the Demon of Benfield. It had more or less said so on the news. Whoever was lurking in the greenery, it was not the killer.

But other men preyed on women and the Demon's crimes might have inspired imitators. They might try to kill but perhaps merely try to frighten. Jenny was moving swiftly when she realized she had made a bad mistake.

Miles saw the magenta blob slow down. Then he had an unobstructed view of her because she had come to the edge of the burned area. She had run out of cover. To gain the main path she had to cross the blackened patch where movement among the burned hulks and fallen trees was treacherously difficult. Miles's hand was white-knuckled around the wooden stave as he waited to see what she would attempt.

Jenny sensed her pursuer watching her choose her next move. She had a degree of safety while she stood there because he did not want to reveal himself. The pause gave her time to think. She believed that in a hand-to-hand tussle she could cope with him and she would have the advantage because he would not expect that. But by then he would have attacked and she wanted a way of preventing it. She decided the sensible thing was to let him see she was armed. She picked up a strong length of wood, hoping he understood she was capable of using it. If she got the opportunity.

Then she turned left, towards the vicarage. She skirted the charred area, going fast, watching her footing, not wasting precious seconds on backward glances. Someone was crashing along behind her. He had given up any pretence that she was not being followed. He was aiming to rush up behind her and bludgeon her.

Miles knew that at Jenny's increased speed she would soon reach the safety of the vicarage garden. He had to get to her. Never mind whether she saw him, *he had to to it*. He rehearsed his reasons for hating her. Her interference. Her patronizing ways. Her plan to reveal he was at the cottage and the consequent threat the police would find out what he had done.

It was unfair. He had come to Benfield for a fresh start. Jenny was the one who had made things go awry. And then that girl had come, the one he mistook for the woman who pestered him at the last place he lived. He had followed her from the church, right down the Harpury road and into the field. That was his chance and he had grabbed it. He did not know it was all a mistake until the radio had said it was not her at all, it was somebody called Mary Cross.

He hated women. They would never leave him alone. That Susan Dawlish, the one who was so stupid she thought she was in Ayot wood when she was in Benfield wood, invaded his camp. And Veronica Long, always chattering at him, spied on him too. He hated them all. He lunged after Jenny.

A fallen tree delayed her. Jenny's head was full of the noise of her pursuer thundering towards her. She gave a cry and spun round, her weapon held across her in a defensive gesture. She never had a greater shock in her life than when she saw Jeffrey Miles. *Jeff!* It ought to have been all right, it was only Jeff. But she knew it was not all right. This was Miles as she could not have imagined him, in a demonic rage. There was a flame in those normally dispassionate eyes which she had never seen in any sane person's eyes. He was raising high above his head a great piece of wood and coming at her. Irrelevantly she recognized his weapon as the strut she had failed to fix on Mrs Pendle's gate. And then she was over the obstacle and backing from him.

Flight or fight? Now it had come to it she did not hesitate. Clever throws and tricky footwork were no match for an armed assailant with the strength of a madman. Jenny fled.

Miles saw through the red glow of his rage the astonishment on Jenny's face when she recognized who had come to kill her. If she had not been so fit and agile he would have had her then, by the fallen tree. Instead he had to go after her, a desperate energy propelling him. His body was numb to the pain of scratches and knocks as he hurtled after her. The weight of the stave was no impediment. And then Jenny slipped.

Jenny slipped where a long-fallen branch had become brittle. Instinctively she rolled away as she hit the ground. The crash beside her was the first of the blows Miles struck. She scrambled up, getting away from him but unable to avoid a burned clearing where confrontation was inevitable. When she went down she had lost her weapon. There was nothing to hand which was not uselessly friable. She jinked backwards, like a boxer drawing her opponent forward. But there were no ropes to lean on, no referee. She was delaying the moment when he killed her. She drew him into the clearing, thinking hysterically that at last she had got Jeffrey Miles out into the open, at last she understood him. Neither of them said a word. High overhead rooks wheeled and pigeons murmured. In the clearing there was the sound of harsh breathing, feet scuffling and the rush of air as Miles aimed blows.

Jenny timed: 'The *next* blow. No, the one *after*. That thing is heavy. It must wear him out a bit.' But it did not. His blows did not get weaker. He had an energy which took no account of normal human frailty, of the limitations of muscle and sinew. So she waited for another blow and as he swung the murderous piece of wood she was poised. Immediately it reached the lowest point of its arc, before he could begin to raise it again, Jenny threw herself on him.

She went for the throat, a primitive instinct which, when all the fancy theories have been tested, is as good as anything. Technique and the lessons of the gymnasium did not matter to her because the throat is vulnerable, accessible.

Miles was flattened. Jenny kicked the stave away and fought for her breath while waiting for him to get up. She planned to knock him out and run for the police at the vicarage.

He began to rise. She swung out a foot and he went down. Jenny ripped off her cotton belt ready to tie his hands before he recovered. She got near but he had fooled her. He sprang up and grabbed her. Although she wrested her arm from his grip he ripped the belt away. He came after her, the magenta strip held between his hands. She was being forced back into impenetrable foliage. They both knew that when he closed on her he would throttle her with her own belt.

She flew at him again but the ground made her movements unsure and she could not get him down. They grappled, neither succeeding until Jenny felt the belt against her neck. Seconds later she threw him, tumbling on top of him because he did not release his grip on the cloth. With a tremendous effort she wrenched herself free, leaving him on the ground, winded and holding the belt limply.

In the corner of her eye she saw the stave from the gate and went for it. Miles was trying to rise when she ran back with the weapon. Their eyes met as she raised it above her head with both hands and prepared to smash it down on his skull, to kill.

The blow never landed. Jenny was grabbed from behind by her husband and a policeman.

31

In the small hours of the night the Reverend Adam King went into his church. He carried a cold chisel and a hammer.

He came out again as first light through the east window stained the nave with subdued colours. And he was in bed by the time shadows lifted from the medieval saints and a ravaged panel whose subject was no longer identifiable.

Jeffrey Miles's guilt at destroying the serpent of St John the Evangelist was never questioned. King had no qualms about letting him carry the blame. It was the solution to two problems. There need be no controversy about covering the basilisk again and no embarrassment at King's innocence in failing to recognize evil.

Later that morning he telephoned Jenny's cousin, Donald Gill, and asked how much he knew about Miles. Gill hedged before admitting he had been told Miles had suffered periods of mental illness and was discharged from hospital the previous winter. The friend who recommended Miles thought he got severe depressions, at any rate he tended to be withdrawn and moody.

'It didn't seem fair to mention that, Adam. All Jeffrey Miles wanted was some work in a quiet environment and your carvings seemed ideal.' He laughed. 'Taking him on was an unwitting act of charity on your part.'

At last it occurred to him to ask: 'Why? Nothing's happened, has it?'

A child's sock lay on a bedroom floor, overlooked when clothes and toys had been stuffed into bags. Sheila's parents had swooped and carried his family away.

Dale drank a lager, listening to the aching silence of the house and understanding that it would deepen as the days dragged on. Bewildered by the sudden retraction of Welford's accusations, he had come home, not to relief, but to desolation.

Very early next morning he went to Brigges, wrote his resignation, took the photograph from his desk and handed his car to the security man. By the time his colleagues learned he had been charged with pornography and dog fighting, he would have passed out of their lives. As he left the building he felt utterly free.

He never knew the irony that Pauline Williams resigned later that month. Her flatmate wanted to spend her convalescence with friends in Italy and Pauline was to travel with her, then stay and find work there.

Dale got a job with a man running a computer magazine in Bedford. He took to eating his evening meals at pubs on the route home. In one there was a red-haired waitress, no more than twenty, with the milky complexion redheads have if they are lucky. Dale told her he was a photographer, gave his name as Williams and asked whether she was interested in a career as a model.